Arafel had taken little with her out of otherwhere, and yet did take: it was always in the eye which saw her. She had come as plainly as ever she had ventured into the mortal world, and leaned against the rotting trunk of a dying tree and folded her arms without a hint of threat, laying no hand now to the silver sword she wore. More, she propped one foot against a projecting root and offered him her thinnest smile, much out of the habit of smiling at all.

The boy looked on her with no less apprehension for that effort, seeing, perhaps, a ragged vagabond in outlaw's habit—or perhaps seeing more and having more reason to fear, because he did not look to be as blind as some.

His hand touched a talisman at his breast and she, smiling still, touched that pale green stone which hung at her own throat, a talisman which had power to answer his. . . .

T·H·E
DREAMSTONE

C.J. Cherryh

DAW BOOKS, INC.
DONALD A. WOLLHEIM, PUBLISHER

1633 Broadway, New York, NY 10019

Cover art by David A. Cherry.

Substantially different versions of portions of this book appeared as *The Dreamstone*, published in *Amazons*, DAW Books, 1979, and as *Ealdwood*, published by Donald M. Grant, 1981.

DAW Book Collectors No. 521.

FIRST PRINTING, MARCH 1983

5 6 7 8 9

PRINTED IN THE U.S.A.

CONTENTS

BOOK ONE • THE GRUAGACH

BOOK TWO • THE SIDHE

BOOK ONE

The Gruagach

ONE

Of Fish and Fire

Things there are in the world which have never
loved Men, which have been in the world far
longer than humankind, so that once when
Men were newer on the earth and the woods
were greater, there had been places a Man
might walk where he might feel the age of the
world on his shoulders. Forests grew in which
the stillness was so great he could hear stir-
rings of a life no part of his own. There were
brooks from which the magic had not gone,
mountains which sang with voices, and sometimes a wind touched the back of his neck and
lifted the hairs with the shiver of a presence at
which a Man must never turn and stare.

But the noise of Men grew more and more
insistent. Their trespasses became more bold.
Death had come with them, and the knowledge

of good and evil, and this was a power they had, both to be virtuous and to be blind.

Axes rang. Men built houses, and holds, rooted up stone, felled trees, made fields where forests had stood from the foundation of the world; and they brought bleating flocks to guard with dogs that had forgotten they were wolves. Men changed whatever they set hand to. They wrought their magic on beasts, to make them dull and patient. They brought fire and the reek of smoke to the dales. They brought lines and order to the curve of the hills. Most of all they brought the chill of iron, to sweep away the ancient shadows.

But they took the brightness too. It was inevitable, because that brightness was measured against that dark. Men piled stone on stone and made warm homes, and tamed some humbler, quieter things, but the darkest burrowed deep and the brightest went away, heartbroken.

Save one, whose patience or whose pride was more than all the rest.

So one place, one untouched place in all the world remained, a rather smallish forest near the sea and near humankind, keeping a time different than elsewhere

Somewhen this forest had ceased to be a lovely place. Thorns choked it, beyond its fringe of bracken. Dead trees lay unhewn by any woodman, for none would venture there. It was

THE GRUAGACH

a perilous place by day. By night it felt far worse, and a man did well not to build a fire too near the aged trees. Things whispered here, and the trees muttered with the wind and perhaps with other things. Men knew the place was old, old as the world, and they never made peace with it.

But on a certain night a man was weary, and he had seen very much of horror and of the world's hard places, so that a little fire to cook by seemed a very small hazard against others he had run this day, the matter of a few twigs to cook a bit to eat.

He had come and gone a great deal on the banks of the river Caerbourne and in the fringes of this forest, for five whole years. If there were outlaws hereabouts he knew them all by name. And if there were other dangers he had never met them, so they failed to frighten him, this night, and on other nights when he had come this far beneath the aged boughs and heard the rustlings and the whisperings of the leaves. He made his little fire and cooked his fish and ate it, which seemed to him like a feast after his famine of recent days. He felt home again; he felt safe; he looked forward to a bed among the leaves where no two-legged enemy would be likely to come on him.

But Arafel had noticed him.

* * *

She had little interest in the doings of Men in general. Her time and her living were very much different from the years of humankind, but she had seen this Man before as he slipped about the margins of her wood. He was deft about it and did no harm, and he was wary and hard for harm to come to: such a Man never quite disturbed her peace.

But this night he took a fish from the Caerbourne's stream and built a fire to cook it, beneath an ancient oak. And this was far too great a familiarity.

So she came. She stood watching for a while unnoticed in her gray hooded cloak, in the shadows among the oaks. The Man had had his fish, leaving only the naked bones in the fire, and now knelt, cherishing the warmth of the tiny flame and heap of ash, cupping his hands close above it. He was rough-looking, with a weathered countenance and gray-streaked hair—a lean and weary Man with the taint of iron about his person, for a sword lay close beside his knee. She had been apt to anger when she came, but he sat so small and quiet for so tall a Man, clinging to so small a warmth in the great dark of the wood, that she wondered at him, how he had come, or why, presuming so much for so little comfort. She was not the first to come. The shadows moved beyond his little fire and hissed in indignation. He never seemed to notice, deaf to them and blinded by the light he clung to.

THE GRUAGACH

"You should take more care," she said.

He snatched at his great sword and came to one knee all in one motion.

"No," she said quietly, moving forward. "No, I am quite alone coming here. I saw your fire."

The sword stayed half-drawn across his knee. He had heard nothing, seen nothing until now. A gray-mantled figure showed like a trick of moonlight in the thicket, so dim even the tiny fire might have blinded his eyes, but he had no excuse at all for his ears. "Who are you?" he asked. "Of An Beag, would you be?"

"No. Of this place. I rarely stir out of it. Put the sword away."

He was off his balance and not accustomed to that. Why he was sitting still at all instead of standing sword in hand was not quite clear to him, only that there had never seemed a moment of clear decision since the stranger started speaking. The voice was smooth and fair. He could not get the timbre of it in his mind, whether it was young or old or what it was even when it was just dying in the air, no more than he could make out the figure in the dark, but he found he had slid the sword back into its sheath, not having clearly decided to put it back at all. His hands were cold. "Share if you like," he said, with a motion toward the fire. "The warmth, at least. If it's food you want, catch your own. I've eaten all I had."

"I have no need." The stranger came nearer, so silently no leaf whispered and settled at the side of the tiny clearing on the dead log that fended the wind from his fire. "What would your name be?"

"Give me yours," he said.

"I have many."

Little by little the chill of the ground had come creeping up to him, and now the fire between them seemed all too dim and small. "And what would one of them be?" he asked, because he was always a man to want answers even when they were ill.

"I have marked your coming and going hereabouts." The answer came so still and soft the rustle of a leaf might have overcome it. "Other things have seen you, do you not know? Your step was always soft and quick until tonight; but now you settle in to stay—is that your hope? No, I think not. I do think not. You are wiser than that."

She saw the hardness of his face as he stared at her. It was a face which might well have been fair once, but years and scars had marred it; and sun and wind had weathered it, so that it was fit for the rest of him, with ragged hair and ragged clothes and dark, hopeless eyes. As for him, there was no knowing what he saw of her: Men saw what they pleased to see, often as not. Perhaps to him she was some outlaw like himself or some great mail-clad warrior from over the river. His hand never let go the sword.

"Why do you come?" she asked him last.

THE GRUAGACH

"For shelter."

"What, in *my* wood?"

"Then I will leave your wood, as quickly as I may."

"There is harm outside this circle—No, it would not be well to look just now. As for the fish and the fire, both are costly. And what will you offer me for them?"

He gave no answer. If there was any wealth he had besides the sword itself she could not tell it. And that he did not offer.

"What," she said, "nothing?"

"What will you have?" he asked.

"Truth. For the fish and the fire tell me truly what you do in my woods."

"I live."

"No more than that? It seems to be a hard living. There's a sorrow about you, Man. Is there ever joy?"

This was baiting. The Man felt it, and felt his weariness hovering over him like urging sleep. There was peril in that sleep, and that he also knew. He set the cap of his sheathed sword on the ground and leaned heavily on it, looking at the stranger, trying to look more closely, but his sight seemed to dim whenever he looked hardest, and some fold of the cloak was always casting a shifting shadow just where he looked, so that he could see nothing that was beneath it. He knew beyond a doubt that he had met one of the fair folk, and he knew it though the moment was moonbeams and shadows and something his eyes refused to see. He had never expected such a meeting in his life, being occupied with his own business, but he knew it when it was on him and understood his danger, that the fair folk were fell and deadly with trespassers, and given to dark mischief. But perhaps it was part of the binding on him that he felt no reticence at all with this stranger, as if it were the last night of the world and the last friend had come to listen. "I have come here," he said, "sometimes. It seemed safe. I brought no enemy here. An Beag would never follow."

"Why do they hunt you?"

"I am a King's man."

"And they have some quarrel with this King?"

The voice seemed innocent, fair as a child's. The years went reeling back and back for him and he leaned the more heavily on the hilt of his sword, aching in all his bones, and laughed. "Quarrel, aye. They killed the King at Aescford, burned Dun na h-Eoin—now there is no king at all. Five years gone—" He grew hoarse in telling it. It was incredible to him that all the world was not shaken by that fall, but the figure before him stayed unmoved.

"Wars of Men. They are nothing to me. The fish matters. That touches my boundaries."

A chill wandered up his back, but dimly through his remembered grief. "So, but I gave you the truth for it."

"That was the price I named. Now I give you good advice: do not come again." The shadow rose, graying into dark. "This once I will guide you to the river, but only once."

He leaned on the sword and levered himself to his feet as if it were the last strength he had; and perhaps it was. His shoulders were bowed. His head was down for the moment, but then it lifted, and he pointed another way with a straightening of his shoulders. "Give me leave to go along the shore. A mile or so down the river I can slip my enemies and I will go as quickly as I can."

"No. You must go as you came, and now."

"So," he said, and bent and patiently covered up his fire, then took up his sword, half drawing it although in his eyes was no hope at all. "But my enemies are waiting there, and whatever you are, I will make a beginning here if I have no choice. I ask you again—let me pass along the shore. I was always a good neighbor to this wood. I never set axe to it. I beg your courtesy this once. It is so small a thing."

She considered him, so soft-spoken, so set upon his way. Almost she went fading back again and leaving this Man to the dark and the night. But there was no dark anger in him, only the sadness of something brave that once had been. So the old stag died, among the wolves; or the eagle fell; or the wolf himself went down. She thought a moment and thinking on such a heart remembered a place, a small place, the only warmth she knew among humankind.

"I shall tell you a way to go," she said gently, "and help you come to it if perhaps you can, a place deep in the hills and not so perilous as my lands. But you must come with me now step for step and never stray: Death has been very near to you tonight. He is very skillful at stalking, more than any Man. No, never look. Come now, come, put away the sword and follow. Follow me."

A second time he slid the sword back into its sheath and never felt the doing of it; he walked as once he had walked after bloody Aescford, out of the hills, aware first of fending branches from his face and then that he had come some distance never remembering any of it; and that he was lost. He was well-schooled in woodcraft and no man could have eluded him so close at hand, but the gray cloak melted through the thickets before him as if the branches had no substance, and though he went as quickly as he could, he could never come near his guide. He was panting, and his heart labored with a beating he could hear, so loud it dimmed all other sounds. Branches raked his face and arms. Leaves whipped past with a soft and clinging touch.

But at last the stranger waited for him on the river bank, standing against a very aged tree, so that the gray cloak might have been part of the bark in the moonlight. They had come to the widest part of the Caerbourne,

THE GRUAGACH

where it flowed most shallowly: he knew it, every stone along the shore.

And his guide pointed him the way across.

"This is the ford," he objected. "And they will be watching it."

"They are not. Not this while. Perhaps not again for several nights—trust me that I know. Yonder you see the hills, and atop the first hill is a cairn; and beneath the second as you follow the river course from the narrows below the cairn, there go up the dale and up the farther hill. The place I send you, you will never see it, except you come up the dell and over against the shoulder of the Raven's Hill . . . do they call it that, these days?"

"That is still the name." He looked toward the shadowy line of hills beyond the river, beyond the trees. The river water danced with a light that broke beside him. He turned his head in alarm toward his companion. There was no one there, as if there had never been, only the fading memory of a voice of a high, fair tone, as he had never heard it, and the recollection of a light he had almost seen.

The world seemed dark then, and cold, and the shadows full of menace.

"Are you there ?" he asked the dark, but nothing answered.

He shivered then, and slinging his sword at his back, waded the Caerbourne's chill flood up to his waist, constantly expecting arrows from out of the dark trees on the other side, ambush and after all, the chill laughter of the fair folk at his back. There was no luck in faery-gifts. He doubted all his safety now, forever.

But nothing started on that shore except a small splash that swam away into the reeds, and he climbed out again on the side of the river his enemies held, finding no one watching, and no harm near him. He began at once to run to keep the warmth in his legs, dodging along among the few young trees which grew on the naked borders of An Beag and its villages.

He was Niall, lately called Dubhlachan and formerly other names, who had been a lord in years gone by; but the King he served now was a helpless babe hidden somewhere in the hills— so loyal hearts believed. And the loyal men lived and harried the traitors' fields in Caerbourne vale and elsewhere as they could, which was all they could do till the young King should live to be a man.

Five years Niall had lived in the forest edges, under stone and hidden in thickets, and men had followed him, but most were dead and the rest now scattered.

So he ran, ran at last because the sun was coming, and ran because a dream in the dark wood had promised safety. He was not young any longer. He had lost all his faith in kings to come. It was only a fireside he wanted, and bread to eat, and no more hunt at his heels.

THE GRUAGACH

*　　*　　*

The sun came up on him and still he ran by turns, coming up into the Brown Hills. Men called them haunted, like the wood. But he had long had the habit of such places, where no comfortable men would go. The rumor only gave him hope, more and more as he came among the hills. Weariness left him, so that he ran more lightly than he had run before, through the rough stones and the desolation. The sun was on him. The sweat ran. He heard his steps fall and jar the stones together, but nothing more in all the world, as if some veil lay on his senses and the world had stopped being what it was. If the forest had been dark, this was bright, and the sun danced here, and the stones shone in the light.

He reached the Raven's Hill and climbed. A strangeness glistened under the nooning sun, under the shoulder of the opposing hill. And so he ran, ran, ran, with a great expectation in his heart, and if he began to die in that running, still he drove himself with the hope of something, some barrier to cross, some place one only got to by chance or luck or the last hope in all the world.

It was a homely place, of fields and fences, stone and golden thatch and a crooked chimney, and the smell of bread baking, and the sun shining on the barley round about and on the dust.

"Come see, come see!" he heard someone call as he fell to his knees and full length on the ground. "O come! here's a man come fallen in the yard!"

TWO

Beorc's Steading

The sweat ran in rivulets on Niall's back, and it was a good feeling, swinging a mallet and not a sword, driving the pegs in just so, to mend the grain-bin before the new harvest came in, the fields standing golden white in the sun.

A dour-faced boy brought him water: he dipped up enough to drink and poured the rest over his head, blinking in the stream, and the boy Scaga took the dipper back and sulked off about his rounds, but that was ever Scaga's manner and no one minded. Birds lighted on the fencepost when the boy had gone, cocked wise eyes at Niall, darted down to peck a bit of grain from the dust as he turned back to work again. Dinner was foremost in his mind, one of Aelfraeda's fine hearty dinners set beneath the evening sky as they ate in summertime, beneath the spreading oak that shaded the Steading; some would sing and some would listen, and so the stars would light them to bed until the sun waked them out of it.

That was the way of the days at Beorc's Steading, and Beorc himself ordered matters in all this wide farm so that no days were idle and everything was done in its season, like the mending before the harvest. There were full two score hands to work, men and women and children. The fields were wide, and the orchards likewise, and the sheep grazed the hill by the spring while the cattle and the pony pastured down by the tiny brook it made. There gnarled willows shaded time-rounded stones and a child could wade most of it. Closer, where the brook came nearest the barn, lived a herd of fat pigs and a flock of geese as fat as the pigs and noisier, who bullied their way about the farm. But also about the hillside there was a wolf, a well-fed and lazy cub who liked ear-scratching; and a fawn who strayed in and nosed her way everywhere. A badger had his hole in the hollow next the turnip field; and a host of birds lived round about, from the heron who lived on the brook to the family of owls who lived in the barn. They were all lostlings. They had all come like the cub and the fawn and fallen under the peace Aelfraeda maintained. There was such a spell on them they never preyed on each other, except the heron

THE GRUAGACH

fished the brook and the owls had the barn
mice who minded no laws at all.

This extended to the two-footed kind—for
they all had come, excepting Beorc and Aelfraeda themselves, as lostlings themselves, both
old and young, and none were kin at all. There
was old grandfather Sgeulaiche, as wizened
and withered as last winter's apple, whose hands
and clever blade turned out the most marvelous things of wood, who sat on the porch in a
pool of sweet smelling curls of wood and told
stories to whatever girl or boy who was set to
work the churn or card the wool—for there
were children here, half a dozen of them, no
one's and everyone's, like the fawn. There was
of course half-grown Scaga, who pilfered food
at every chance and hid it, though Aelfraeda
would have given him both hands full of anything he asked—he fears being hungry, Aelfraeda said; so, let him hide all he will, and
eat all he can—someday he will smile. There
was Haesel hardly six and Holen more than
twelve; and Siobrach and Eadwulf and Cinhil
in between. Of adults there was Siolta, who
was lame and in middle years, who baked and
made wonderful cheeses, and there was Lonn
who had a great swordcut running from brow
to chin and many others beside, but his hands
were sure and good with the cattle: Siolta and
Lonn were man and wife, though never they
had known each other before this place. There
was Conmhaighe and Carraig and Cinnfhail

and Flann; and Diomasach, Diarmaid and the other Diarmaid; and Ruadh; and Fitheach and the other men and women, so that there were never workers lacking for the hardest tasks inside the house or out, besides Beorc and Aelfraeda themselves, who were wherever work wanted doing, cheerful and foremost in any task

In all, the weather blessed the place and the grain grew tall and the green apples grew round and fine; and the brook never failed in summer. There was a haze of light about the hills by daylight, so that it made the eyes sting to try to look into the distance of the Brown Hills; and the mountain shoulder lay between the Steading and the river away to the south, and between it and the harrying of An Beag and other names which seemed a dream here.

"Do you not set a guard?" Niall had asked of Beorc early, while they had tended him in the house and fed him until he was less gaunt than before. "Do you not have men to watch the way to this place? I would do that. Weapons are what I know."

But, "No," Beorc had said, and his face, broad and plain and ruddy, had creased with laughter. "No. You had luck to come here. Few are lucky, and them I welcome. So there is a great deal of luck on this valley of mine. If you will stay, stay: if you will go, I will show you a way to go, but if you turned around again after, I do not

think your luck would find the place a second
time."

Then Niall said nothing more of boundaries
and borders, perceiving some force in Beorc
that kept its own limits and expected everything about him to do likewise. He is, Niall
had thought then with a queer kind of shiver,
more like a king than not. And king did not fit
Beorc either, with his wispy nimbus of gray-
red hair, his cheeks wind-burned above a beard
as well and lawless as his mane. Like a fire he
was, a gust of wind, a great broad man who
laughed much and kept his own counsels; and
Aelfraeda was like him and unlike, a woman
of strong hands and ample girth and beautiful
golden braids coiled crownlike about her head,
who carried her own milkpails, thank you, and
wove and spun and fed strays both two and
four-footed, having the law in her house and
for scepter a wooden spoon.

It was a place that luck smiled on, and in
which more than a usual share of amazing
things happened: for weeds that happened into
the crops turned up in the morning wilted and
limp beside the rows so that hardly ever did
one have to take a hoe to the vegetables; and if
some few vegetables vanished in the same night,
no one spoke of it. Tools one would have sworn
were lost turned up found in the morning on
the porch, fit to set a shiver up a less compla-
cent spine. Likewise the pannikin of milk and
the buttered cakes Aelfraeda faithfully set out

each night on the bench on the porch turned up missing, each and every crumb, which might have been the wolf cub's doing or the fawn's, or the geese, but Niall never spied the cakes vanishing and had no wish to go out of nights to see.

And most peculiar, there was the Brown Man, or so Niall called him, skulking here and there in the orchards, or among the rocks, fit to account for a great deal that was odd hereabouts. "He is very old," said Beorc when Niall reported it. "Never trouble him."

Old he might be, Niall suspected, old as stone and hills and all, for there was something uncanny about him and bespelled. Nothing could move so quickly, coming into the tail of the eye and out again, and skipping away among the rocks. There he sat now, a small brown lump by the barn, barefoot, knees tucked up in arms, and watching, watching the mending of the bin. He was wrinkled as an old man and agile as any child; and his brown hair fell down about his hairy arms and his beard sprayed about his bare and well-thatched chest. His oversized hands and feet were furred just the same. Brown as a nut and no taller than a half-grown boy, with hair wellshot with gray and usually flecked with wisps of straw, he hung about the barn and nipped apples from the barrel and sometimes sat on the pony's back in the stall, feeding him with good apples too.

THE GRUAGACH

And this Brown Man had a way about him of being there one moment and elsewhere in the next, so that when Niall cast him a second look round the corner of the shed he was gone.

On that same instant something prickled his bare back and he spun about with an oath and almost a sweep of the hammer. As quickly as he spun a shadow dived in the corner of his eye and he kept spinning, following it as it nabbed a fistful of grain from the bin: but it was gone, quick as he could turn, and round the corner of the shed. "Hey!" he cried, and hurled himself round the corner, but it was gone a second time, a wisp of brown headed around the corner.

Once he had followed it: he knew better now. It had led him over fences and stones and over the brook and back again. Now he dived back again around the corner and caught it coming round behind him. He flung the mallet, not to hit it, but to scare it.

It screamed and tucked down instead of running. It kept tucked down, its face in its hairy hands, and peered out quickly to see if another mallet was coming.

"Here now," Niall said. "Here." He was suddenly in the wrong and hoping no one had seen.

It ventured another eye above its hands, then spat and scampered off on its short legs.

"Perish it," Niall muttered to himself, and then wished he had not said that either. Noth-

ing went well this day. He left his pegs and his
mallet and followed it to the barn and inside.

Straw showered down his neck. "Plague on
you," he cried, but it went scampering through
the rafters disturbing the owls in a flapping of
wings. "Come back!"

But it was gone and out the door.

"Do not try."

It was Beorc who had come in behind him,
and shame flooded Niall's face. He was not
accustomed to be made sport of or to be caught
in the wrong either. "I would not have hit
him."

"No, but you hurt his pride."

A moment Niall was silent. "What will mend
it?"

"Be kind," said Beorc. "Only be kind."

"Call him back," said Niall in sudden despair.

"That I cannot. He is the Gruagach and no
one has the calling of him: he will never tell
his name."

Niall shivered then, for his luck seemed to
have left him. It will end now, he thought, for
frightening one of the fair folk: he remembered
how he had come to the Steading, and how it
needed luck to find the place and needed luck
to stay.

That night he had no appetite, and set his
dinner on the porch beside the platter Aelfraeda
set out; but in the morning Aelfraeda's gift was
taken and his was left.

Yet there was no certain turning in his luck, except that now and again he had straw dumped on his head when he went into the barn and now and again his tools vanished when his back was turned, to appear on their pegs in the barn when he came hunting others.

All this he bore with patience unlike himself, even setting an especially fine apple out where the theft was returned—which gift vanished: but so, daily, did his tools. All the same he taught himself to smile about it, concealing his misfortune and making little of it, no matter how long the walk.

So great a patience did he achieve that it even extended to the boy Scaga's thefts, so that one day that he came on the boy pilfering his lunch in the field he only stood there, and Scaga looked up with his eyes all round with startlement.

Niall had a mallet in his hand this day too, but he kept it in his hand. "Will you not leave a morsel?" he asked. "I've been hard at my work."

The boy looked at him, down on his haunches as he was and ill-set for running. And he set the basket down.

"Will you have half?" Niall asked the boy. "I'd like the company."

"There's not much," the red-haired rascal said, looking doubtfully under the napkin.

"There's always enough to give half of," Niall said, and did.

It was a silent lunch. Scaga stole from others after, but never from him. And sometimes his tools came back on Scaga's quick legs before he missed them.

One day about that time the Gruagach came and sat and watched him, and he spied it looking round the corner of the barn at him.

"Here," he said, his heart lifting at this approach. He offered a handful from the bin, "here's grain. I've a bit of bread about me if you like. Good cheese." The head vanished before the words had left his mouth. But it lurked about and looked at him and stole his tools only now and again, just to remind him.

His luck lasted, and the days rolled on, from summer heat to harvest: the fawn grew gangling and the wolf cub yelped at the moon of nights; and the sickles turned up sharpened on their own each harvest morning.

But one nooning a man came stumbling up the valley from the south, off the shoulder of Raven's Hill, startling the geese.

Niall came as all the house came running. The man had fallen trying to cross the fence, a bony huddle of limbs and weapons, for he carried a bow and an empty quiver, a sword at his side. Lonn had caught him up and held him, and so Niall came, and stopped and fell to his knees in dismay, because he knew this man. "His name is Caoimhin," Niall said. A fear had come on him as if all his safety wavered. For the briefest moment he looked beyond the fences, where the folding hills trapped his sight, half-expecting to see pursuit coming hard on Caoimhin's heels. But then he felt a hand close on his and looked down in shame

"Lord," Caoimhin said, and his hand trembled in its grip on his, Caoimhin, best of bowmen they had had. "O my lord, we heard that you were dead."

"No," said Niall, "hush, be still, lean on me: I'll help you walk."

Caoimhin let him lift him up, trusting only him, clinging most to him and leaning on him, so with Beorc and Lonn and Flann and Carraig and all the troop they brought him into the yard, and so into the house and Aelfraeda's care, than which there was none better.

It was broth that day and bread and butter, but Caoimhin limped as far as the porch in the evening, and then to the yard where the table groaned with food beneath the oak, and the harvesters came singing home. Having gotten that far he only stared with that far lost look of a man too hard for tears, but Niall came to rescue him and Beorc clapped him heartily on the shoulder and called for a cup of ale for him, and another plate at table.

"Here," Niall bade Caoimhin quickly, and gave up his own seat until everyone rearranged themselves and Siolta brought a dish and cup for him. "He is Caoimhin," Beorc said, lifting

his cup to him. So they all did, and fell to one
of Aelfraeda's grand good meals.

Caoimhin tried, a bit of this and that, but
his hands shook and at last he sat there with
the tears running down his face and a bit of
bread in his hand. But Niall put his arm about
him and held him in his place, he was so weak,
and if the company grew quiet a moment, they
understood and the merriment picked up again.
"What is this place?" Caoimhin asked when he
had had a sip of ale.

"Refuge," said Niall. "And safety. A place
where ill has never been. And never shall."

"Are we dead then?"

"No," Niall laughed. "Never dead."

But a niggling fear was on him. He even
wished Caoimhin had never come, because this
man reminded him what he had been, and
brought the stink of death about him. More, he
was afraid for the peace of all this place, as if
it had taken some great danger to its heart.

Caoimhin lay about the house the next few
days, or rested on the porch in the sunlight
and the breeze, and slept much and drank and
ate wholesome food when he waked, so that his
face looked less haggard and less desperate.

In those first days he wanted at least his
sword by him and kept it by him even napping
in the sun. And ever and again his hand would
stray to find it in his sleep, and his fingers curl
about the sheath or hilt, so his face would lose

its moment's trouble and he would rest again. But on the third day he let it go; and the fourth he walked out of the house and left it behind, beside the hearth with his bow and his empty quiver. So he sat with old Sgeulaiche on the porch and finally strolled about the yard and out to the threshing.

There Niall saw him and wiped the sweat and the dust from his brow and came over to him.

"What," Niall said lightly, "does Aelfraeda know you've strayed?"

"By your leave—"

Niall's brows drew down. "No. Not mine. Not here."

"My lord—"

"No lord, I say. No longer—Caoimhin." He clapped him gently on the shoulder. "Come aside with me."

Caoimhin walked with him, as far as the barn and into the shadow inside, and there Niall stopped. "There is no lord in the Steading," Niall said at once, "if not Beorc himself; no lady if not Aelfraeda. And that is well enough with me. Forget my name."

"I have rested. I am well enough to go back again—I will bring you word again. There are men of ours in the hills—"

"No. No. If you leave this place I do not think you will find it again."

The eagerness died in Caoimhin's lean face. From toe to crown Caoimhin looked at him and seemed to doubt what he saw as if it were his first clear look. "You have got calluses on your hands and not from the sword, my lord. There is straw in your hair. You do a farmer's work."

"I do it well. And I have more joy of it than anything ever I did. And I will tell you there is more good in it than ever I have hoped to do. Caoimhin, Caoimhin, you will see. You will see what this place is."

"It has cast a spell on you, that much I see. The King—"

"The King." A shudder came over Niall and he turned away. "My King is dead; the other— who knows? Who knows if he even exists? I saw my King dead. The other I never saw. A babe smuggled away at night—and who knows whose babe? Some serving maid's? Some beggar's child? Or any child at all."

"I have seen him!"

"So you have seen him. And what proof is that? Any child, I say."

"A boy—a fair blond boy. Laochailan son of Ruaidhrigh, like him as a boy could be. He has five years now. Taithleach keeps him safe— would you doubt *his* word?—always on the move through the hills, so that the traitors will never find him, and they need you now—They need you, Niall Cearbhallain."

"A boy." Niall sat down on the grain bin and looked up at Caoimhin with the taste of ashes in his mouth. "And what am I, Caoimhin? I

THE GRUAGACH

was forty and two when I began to serve this hope of a King to come; and my joints ache, Caoimhin, with five years' sleeping under tree and stone. And if this boy ever comes to take Dun na h-Eoin—look at me. Twenty years it will need to make a boy a man; and how many more to make that man a king? Am I likely to see it done?"

"So, well—and who of the men dead on Aescford field will ever see him king? Or shall I? Or shall I? I do not know. But I do what I can as we always did. Where is your heart, Cearbhallain?"

"Broken. Long ago. I will hear no more of it. *No more.* You'll go or you'll stay as you wish, when you can. But stay for now. Rest. Only a little time. And see what things are here. O Caoimhin—leave me my peace."

A long time Caoimhin was silent, looking desolate and lost.

"Peace," Niall repeated. "Our war is done. There is the harvest; the apples are ripening; there'll be the long wintertime. And no need of swords and no help at all we can be. It's all for younger men. If there's to be a king, he will be theirs, not ours. If we have begun, others will finish. And is that not the way of things?"

"Lord," Caoimhin whispered softly; and then a sudden alarm came into his eyes at a quiet scurrying, a shadow by the door. Caoimhin sprang and hit the door and hurled the listener in the dust. "Here are spies," Caoimhin cried, and nabbed the brown man by the hair and hauled him back struggling and gasping as he was and slammed the door

"Let it go," Niall said at once, "let it go."

Caoimhin had a look at it and flung his right hand back with an oath and an outcry, for it bit him and scratched and clawed, but he held it with the left. "This is no man, this—"

"Gruagach is his name," Niall said, and took Caoimhin's hand from the brown man. The creature hugged Niall's arm and danced behind him and fled, peering out again from the refuge of a pile of hay, with straw and dust clinging all over its hair.

"Wicked, wicked," it said, a voice as slight as itself, that lifted the hairs on a man's neck.

"He will never hurt you," Niall promised it. Never had he heard it speak, though others said it could. "Open the door, Caoimhin—open it! Let it go!"

Carefully Caoimhin pushed at the door and light flooded in. The Gruagach stirred himself and sidled that way, closer than ever Niall had seen him clearly, face seamed and brown and bearded, eyes lightless as deep water peering out from under matted hair. It looked up at him and bobbed as if it bowed on its thick legs. And then it fled, scuttling out as quick as the breeze, and was gone.

Then Niall looked toward Caoimhin, and saw the dread there, and all the surmise. "There is no harm in it."

THE GRUAGACH

"Is there none?" Caoimhin leaned against the door. "Now I know where the cakes go at night, and what the luck is in this place. Come away, Cearbhallain, come *now*."

"I will never go. No. You do not know—the way of this place. Come, a bargain with me— only a little time. You would always take my word. Stay. You can always leave—but you will never find the way back again. Was it ill luck brought you here? Tell me that. Or tell me whether you would be breathing the air this morning or eating a good breakfast and looking forward to dinner. There's no dishonor in being alive. It's not our war any longer. It was our luck that brought us here; it was— perhaps something won. I think so. Think on it, Caoimhin. And stay."

A long time Caoimhin reflected on it, and at last looked at the ground and at last looked at him. "There's autumn ahead," Caoimhin said, weakening.

"And winter. There is winter, Caoimhin."

"Till the spring," Caoimhin said. "In the spring I'll go."

The apples went into the bins; the sausages went to smoke; the oak tree shed his leaves and deep snow drifted down. The Gruagach sat on the roof by the chimney and left prints by the step where the cakes and mulled ale disappeared; and of nights he kept the pony and the oxen company.

"Tell us tales," young Scaga said, as all the household sat about the fire. Marvelous to say, Scaga had taken to making the pony's mash this winter without being asked; and never a thing had been missed about the house since summer. He had, from being last and least, become a thoughtful if sober lad, and attached himself to Niall's side and by adoption, to Caoimhin's as well.

So Caoimhin told of a winter on the Daur and a storm that had cracked old trees; and Sgeulaiche recalled being lost in such a storm. And after, when the whole house curled up to sleep each in their warm nooks, and Beorc and Aelfraeda in their great close-bed in the loft: "It is a young man's winter," Caoimhin said to Niall whose pallet was near his.

"A young man's war," said Niall.

"They have taken your lands," Caoimhin said, "and mine."

A long time Niall was silent. "I have no heir. Nor ever shall, most likely."

"As for that—" Now the silence was on Caoimhin's side, a very long time. "As for that, well, that is for young men too. Like the winter. Like the war."

And after that Caoimhin said nothing. But in the morning a lightness was on him, as if some weight had passed.

He will stay, Niall thought, taking in his breath. At least one man of all that followed me. And then he put that prideful thought

away, along with *my lord* and *Cearbhallain*
and bundled himself into warm clothes, for
there was winter's work to do, the beasts to
care for. The children fought snowball battles:
Caoimhin joined in, stalking with Scaga round
the barn. Niall saw the stealth, the skill that
Caoimhin taught the boy. A moment the chill got
through: but they were only snowballs, and
the squeals and shouts were only children's
laughter.

The Gruagach perched on the roof, and let
fall a double armful and laughed and ran.

"Ha," it cried, going over the rooftree. "Ha!
Wicked!"

"Wither it!" cried Caoimhin, but the ambush
was sprung and the battle lost in pelting
snowballs.

A moment Niall watched, and turned away,
hearing still the squeals and hearing something else. He turned and looked back to prove
to his ears and eyes what it was he heard, and
succeeded, and went his way.

THREE

The Harper

The harvest had come again. The scythes went
back and forth and left stubble in their wake.
By morning the sheaves appeared all in rows,
neatly tied; so the Gruagach slept a mighty
sleep by day, and ate and ate. A pair of fawns
had come this year, a fledgling falcon, a bittern,
a trio of fox kits and a starved and arrow-shot
piebald mare: such were the fugitives the Steading gathered. Now the falcon was flown, and
the bittern too; the fox kits instead of tumbling
about the porch were beginning to stray toward the margins of the Steading, going the
way of the wolf; and the mare had become fast
friends with the Steading's own pony, grown fat
and sleek on sweet grass and grain. The children were delighted with her and hung gar-
lands about her neck with she contrived to slip

and eat often as not: she ate and ate, and began to frisk about at daybreak as if it were the morning of the world and no war had ever been.

So here is another fled from the madness, Niall thought to himself, and loved the mare for her courage in living. He rode at times bareback and reinless when he had leisure, letting her go where she would through the pastures and the hills. He loved the feeling of riding again, and the mare swished her tail and cantered at times for the joy of it, going where she pleased, from rich pasture to cool brook to hillsides in the sunlight, or home again to stable and grain. Banain, he called her, his fair darling. She would bear him of her own will; or any of the children, or the Gruagach who whispered to her in a way that horses understood. Sometimes she was willing to be bridled and Caoimhin rode when the mood came on him, and others did, but rarely and not so well and not so far, for, as Caoimhin said, she has one love and none of us can win her.

So this year had been even kinder than the first to him. But the year was not done with arrivals.

This last one came singing, blithe as brazen, down the dusty margin of the fields, along the track the cattle took to pasture, a youth, a vagabond with a sack on his back and a staff in his hand and no weapon but a dagger. His

hair was blond to whiteness, and blew about
his shoulders to the time of his walking and
the whim of the breeze.

Hey, he sang, *the winds do blow,*
And ho, the leaves are dying,
And season doth to season go
The summer swiftly flying.

Niall was one that saw this apparition. He
was mending fences, and Beorc was near him,
with Caoimhin and Lonn and Scaga. "Look,"
said Caoimhin, and look they did, and looked
at Beorc. Beorc stopped his work and with hands
on hips watched the lad coming so merrily
down the far hillside, Beorc seeming less per-
plexed than solemn.

"Here's one come walking where he knows
not," Niall said. In a furtive smallness of his
heart it disturbed him that anyone could come
less desperate than himself, than Caoimhin
wounded, than half-starved Banain or the
grounded falcon. It upset all his world that
this place could be gained so casually, by simple accident. And then he thought again on the
meanness of that; and a third time that it was
less than likely

"It be one of the fair folk," said Lonn uneasily.

"No," said Beorc. "That he is not. He has a
harp on his shoulder, and his singing is uncommon fine but he is none of the fair folk."

"Do you know him then?" Niall asked, wishing some surety in this meeting.

THE GRUAGACH

"No," Beorc said. "Not I." There was no man living had sharper eyes or ears than Beorc. He spoke while the boy was well off in the distance and the voice was still unclear. But the song came clearer as they listened, bright and fair, and the boy came walking up to them in no great hurry: there was indeed a harp on his shoulder. It rang as he walked and as he stopped.

"Is there welcome here?" the boy asked.

"Always," said Beorc. "For all that find the way. Have you walked far?"

For a moment there seemed a confusion in the boy's eyes. He half turned as if seeking the way that he had come. "I came on the path. It seemed a short way through the hills."

"Well," said Beorc. "Well, shorter and longer than some. The hills are not safe these days."

"There were riders," said the harper vaguely, pointing at the hills. "But they went off their way and I went mine, and I sing as I walk so they will not mistake me—there is still some respect for a harper, is there not, in the lands about Caer Donn?"

"Ah, if you were seeking Caer Donn you are somewhat off your path."

Now the boy looked afraid—not greatly so, but uneasy all the same. "I had come from Donn. Is this then An Beag's land? I had not thought it reached within the hills."

"Freeheld, this is," said Beorc and laughed, waving an arm at all the steading, the house set on the side of the great hill, the golden-stubbled fields, the orchards, the whole wide valley. "And Aelfraeda, my wife, will give a harper a cup of ale and a place by the fire for the asking. If you've a taste for cakes and honey, that we always have—Scaga, show the lad the way."

"Sir," said the harper, quite courteous in his recovery, and made a bow as respectful as for a lord. He shouldered the strap of his harpcase and went off up the hill with Scaga's leading, not without a troubled glance or two the way he had come, but after a few paces his step was light again and quick.

"You have misgivings," Niall said to Beorc at the harper's back, when he was out of hearing. "You never wondered at me or at Caoimhin. Who is he? Or what?"

Beorc continued to stare after the boy a moment, leaning on the rail, and his face had no laughter in it, none. "Something strayed. Caer Donn, he says. Yet his heart is hidden."

"Does he lie?" asked Caoimhin.

"No," said Beorc. "Do you think a harper could?"

"A harper is a man," said Caoimhin. "And men have been known to lie upon a time."

Beorc turned on Caoimhin one of his searching looks, his beard like so much fire in the wind and his hair blowing likewise. "The world has gotten to be an ill place if that is so. But this one does not. I do not fear that."

THE GRUAGACH

"And what when he goes singing songs of us in An Beag?" asked Caoimhin.

"They may search as they will," said Beorc, and shrugged and took up the rail again. "But we shall have songs for it. Perhaps a whole winter's songs, perhaps not."

And Beorc fell to singing himself, which he would when he wished not to discuss a thing.

"Master Beorc," said Caoimhin, annoyed, but Niall took up the other end of the rail and held it in place in silence, so Caoimhin, scowling still, knelt to set the pole.

That evening there were indeed songs at the table in the yard, beneath the stars. The harper played for them on his plain and battered harp, delighting the children with merry songs made just for them. But there were great songs too. He had made one of the great battle at Aesclinn; he sang of the King and Niall Cearbhallain, while Niall himself looked only at the cup in his hands, wishing the song done. There were tears in many eyes as the harper sang; but Beorc and Aelfraeda sat hand in hand, listening and still, keeping their thoughts to themselves; and Niall sat dry-eyed and miserable until the last chord was struck. Then Caoimhin cleared his throat loudly and offered the harper ale.

"Thank you," the boy said—Fionn, he called himself, and that was all. He drank a sip and struck a thoughtful chord, and let the strings ripple a moment. "Ah," he said, and after a moment let the music die and took up the ale again. He drank and looked up at them with the sweat cooling on his brow, and then gave his attention to the harp again.

> *"The fires are low*
> *The breezes blow*
> *And stone lies not on stone.*
> *The stars do wane*
> *And hope be vain*
> *Till he comes to his own."*

Then a chill came on Niall Cearbhallain, and he clenched tight the cup in his hand, for it meant the boy King.

"That song," said Caoimhin, "is dangerous."

"So," said the harper. "But I am wary where I sing it. And a harper is sacred—is he not?"

"He is not," said Niall harshly and set his cup down. "They hanged Coinneach the king's bard in the court of Dun na h-Eoin, before they pulled the walls down." He stood up to leave the table, and then recalled that it was Beorc's table and Aelfraeda's, and not his to be leaving in any quarrel. "It is the ale," he said then lamely, and sank back into his place. "Sing something less grim, master harper. Sing something for the children."

"Aye," said the harper after a moment of looking at him, and blinked and seemed a moment lost. "I will sing for them."

So the harper did, a lilting, merry song, but it struck differently on Niall's heart. Niall looked toward Aelfraeda and Beorc, a pleading look and, receiving nothing of offense, gathered himself from his bench and went away into the dark, down by the barn, where the music was far away and thin and eerie in the night, and the laughter far.

There he leaned against the rail of the pen and felt the night colder than it had been.

"Singing," piped a voice.

It startled him, thin and strange as it was, coming from the haystack, even if he knew the source of it.

"Mind your business," he said.

"Niall Cearbhallain."

A chill ran through him, that it had somehow gotten his name. "You've been lurking under more haystacks than this," he said. "I'd be ashamed."

"Niall Cearbhallain."

The chill grew deeper. "Let me be."

"Be what, Niall Cearbhallain?"

He shrugged aside, shivering, ready to go off anywhere to be rid of this badgering.

"Feasts at the house," said the Gruagach. "And what for me?"

"I'll see a plate set out for you."

"With ale."

"The largest cup."

The Gruagach rustled out of the haystack and hopped up onto the rail, his shagginess all shot through with bits of straw in the dark. "This harper does not see," said the Gruagach.

"He sits and harps and sometimes it comes clear to him and most times not. Your luck has brought him here, Niall Cearbhallain. He came to you first. He is fey. He is your luck and none of his own."

"What made you so wise?" Niall snapped, dismayed.

"What made you so blind, Man? You came here once yourself with the smell of the Sidhe about you."

He had started to turn away. He stopped and stared, cold to the heart. But the Gruagach bounded off the rail and ran.

"Come back!" he called. "Come back here!"

But the Gruagach never would. He was lost into the dark and gone at least until he came for his cakes and ale.

There was a quieter gathering very late that night, in the hall by the fireside where the harper sat half-drowsing with ale, the harp clasped in his arms and the firelight bathing his face with a kindly glow. Beorc and Aelfraeda, Lonn and Sgeulaiche and Diarmaid, a scattering about the room; and Caoimhin was there when Niall came straying in, thinking the hall at rest.

"Sir," said the harper, who rose and bowed, "I hope there was no distress I gave you."

"None," said Niall, constrained by the courtesy. He bowed, and addressed himself to Aelfraeda. "The matter of the cakes—may I see to it?"

THE GRUAGACH

Aelfraeda gathered herself up and everyone was dislodged. "The harper's tired," she said. "To bed, to bed all." She clapped her hands. Beorc moved and the rest did, and the drowsing harper blinked and settled the more comfortably into his corner.

Niall filled the cup himself and took the plate of cakes out on the porch. "Gruagach," he called softly, but heard and saw nothing. He went inside, as all the house was settling to their rest; and Scaga who had made himself inconspicuous in the corner came out of his hiding.

"Enough," said Niall. "To bed.—*Now*." So Scaga fled.

But over Caoimhin he had no such power. Caoimhin remained, watching him, and the harper's eyes were on him.

"Cearbhallain," said the harper quietly.

"And has *he* told you? And how many know?"

"I knew at the table. I have heard the manner of your face."

"What, that it is foul? That it is graceless?"

"I have heard it said you are a hard man, lord. Among the best that served the King. I saw you once—I was a boy. I saw you stand at table tonight and for a moment you *were* Cearbhallain."

"You are still a boy to my years," Niall snapped. "And songs are very well in their moment. In hall. You were not at Aescford or

Aesclinn. It stank and it was long and loud. That was the battle, and we lost."

"But did great good."

"Did we?" Niall turned his side to him, taking the warmth of the dying fire on his face, and a great weariness came on him. "Be that so. But I am for bed now, master harper. For bed and rest."

"You gather men here. To ride out to Caer Wiell. Is that your purpose?"

It startled him. He laughed without mirth. "Boy, you dream. Ride with what? A haying fork and hoe?"

The harper reached beside him at the bricks of the fireplace, pulled forward an old sheath and sword.

"Dusty, is it not?" said Niall. "Aelfraeda must have missed it."

"If you would take me with you—lord, I can use a bow."

"You are mistaken. You are gravely mistaken. The sword is old, the metal brittle. It is no good any more. And I have settled here to stay."

A pain came over the harper's face. "I am no spy, but a King's man."

"Well for you. Forget Caer Wiell."

"Your cousin—the traitor—"

"Give me no news of him."

"—holds your lands. The lady Meara is prisoned there, his wife by force. The King's own cousin. And you have *settled* here?"

Niall's hand lifted and he turned. The harper had set himself for the blow. He let his hand fall.

"Lord," Caoimhin said.

"If I were the Cearbhallain," said Niall, "would I be patient? He was never patient. As for taking Caer Wiell—what would you, harper? Strike a blow? An untimely blow. Look you, look you, lad—Think like a soldier, only once. Say that the blow fell true. Say that I took Caer Wiell and dealt all that was due there. And how long should I hold it?"

"Men would come to you."

"Aye, oh aye, the King's faithful men would come—to one hold, to the Cearbhallain's name. And begin battle for an infant king—for a power before its time. But An Beag would rise; and Caer Damh—no gentle enemies. Donn is fey and strange and no trust is in them if there is no strong king. Luel's heart is good but Donn lies between, and Caer Damh—No. This is not the year. In ten, perhaps; in two score there may be a man to crown. Maybe you will see that day. But it is not this day. And my day is past. I have learned patience. That is all I have."

For a moment all was silence. An ember snapped within the hearth. "I am Coinneach the king's bard's son," the harper said. "And I saw you at Dun na h-Eoin once, in the court where my father died."

"Coinneach's son." Niall looked at him, and

the cold seemed greater still. "I had not thought you lived."

"I was with the young King—King he is, lord—until I took to the roads. And I have lodged under hedges and among old stones and now and again in Luel and Donn, aye, and An Beag's steadings too, so never name me coward, lord. Two years I have come and gone and not all in safety."

"Stay," Niall said. "Lad, *stay here*. There is no safety else."

"Not I. Not I, lord. This place is asleep. I have felt it more and more, and I have slept places round about Donn that I would never cross again. Leave this place with me."

"No," Niall said. "Neither Caoimhin nor I. You will not listen. Then never think to come back again. Or to live if you once pass the gates of Caer Wiell. Have you thought how much you could betray?"

"Nothing and no one. I have taken care to know nothing. Two years on the road, lord. Do you think I have not thought? Aye, since Dun na h-Eoin I have thought and come on this journey."

"Then farewell, friends' son," Niall said. "Take my sword if it would serve you. Its owner cannot go."

"It is a courteous offer," the harper said, "but I've no skill with swords. My harp is all I need."

"Take or leave it as you will," Niall said. "It

THE GRUAGACH

will rust here." He turned away and went toward his own nook back along the halls. He did not hear Caoimhin follow. He looked back. "Caoimhin," he said. "The lad has a long way to travel. Go to bed."

"Aye," said Caoimhin, and left him.

The harper left before the dawn—quietly, and taking nothing with him that was not his—"Not a bit to eat," Siolta mourned, "nor anything to drink. We should have set it out for him, and him giving us songs till his voice was gone." But Aelfraeda said nothing, only shook her head in silence and put the kettle on.

And all that morning there was a heavy silence, as if merriment had left them, as if the singing had exhausted them. Scaga moped about his tasks. Beorc went down to the barn in silence and took Lonn and others with him. Sgeulaiche sat and carved on something Sgeulaiche understood, an inchoate thing, but the children were out of sorts from late hours and sulked and complained about their tasks. And Caoimhin who had gone down with Beorc never came to his work

So Niall found him, sitting on the bench at the side of the barn where he should have gathered his tools. "Come," said Niall, "the fence is yet to do."

"I cannot stay," said Caoimhin, so all that he

had feared in searching for Caoimhin came tumbling in on him; but he laughed all the same.

"Work is a cure for melancholy, man. Come
on. You'll think better of it by noontime."

"I cannot stay any longer." Caoimhin gathered himself to his feet and met his eyes. "I
shall be taking my sword and bow."

"To what use? To defend a harper? What
will he be saying to An Beag along the way?
—Pray you never notice that great armed man:
he set it on himself to follow me? A fine pair
you would be along the road."

"So I shall follow. A winter I said I would
stay. But you have stolen a year from me. The
boy was right: this place is full of sleep. Leave
it, Cearbhallain, leave it and come do some
good in the world before we end. No more of
this waking sleep, no more of this place."

"Think of it when you are starved again and
cold, or when you lie in some ditch and none to
hear you—o Caoimhin! Listen to me."

"No," said Caoimhin and flung his arms about
him briefly. "O my lord, one of us should go to
serve the King, even if neither sees his day."

Then Caoimhin went striding off toward the
house, never looking back.

"Then take Banain," Niall cried after him.
"And if you have need then give her her head:
she might bring you home."

Caoimhin stopped, his shoulders fallen. "You
love her too much. Give me your blessing, lord.
Give me that instead."

"My blessing then," said Cearbhallain, and watched him go toward the house, which was as much as he cared to see. He turned. He ran, ran as he had run that day long ago, across the fields, as a child would run from something or to something, or simply because his heart was breaking and he wanted no sight of anyone, least of all of Caoimhin going away to die.

He fell down at last high upon the hillside among the weeds, and his side ached almost as much as his heart. He had no tears—saw himself, a grim, lean man the years had worn as they wore the rocks; and about him was the peace the hillside gave; and below him when he looked down was the orchard ripe with apples, the broad meadow pastures, the house with the barn and the old oak. And above him was the sky. And beyond the shoulder of the hill the way grew strange like the glare of rocks in summer noon, the sheen of sun on grass stems, so that his eyes hurt and he looked away and rose, walking along the hill.

Then a doubt came gnawing at him, so that he passed along the ridge looking for some sight of Caoimhin, like a man worrying at a wound. But when he had come on the valley way he saw no one, and knew himself too late.

"Death," said a thin small voice above him on the hill.

Niall looked up in rage at the shaggy creature on the rock. "What would you know, you croaking lump of straw? Starve from now on! Steal all I have, creeping thief, and starve!"

"Evil words for evil, but only one is true."

"A plague on your prophecy."

"Ill and ill."

"Leave me."

The Gruagach hopped down from the rock and came nearer still. "Not I."

"Will he die then?"

"Perhaps."

"Then be clear." Hope had started up in him, a guilty desperate thing, and he seized the Gruagach by its shaggy arms and held it. "If you have the Sight, then See. Tell me—tell me—was there truth in the harper? Is there hope at all? If there was hope—will there be a King again? Is it on me to serve this King?"

"Let go!" it cried. "Let go!"

"Be plain with me," Niall said and shook it hard, for a terror made him cruel, and the creature's eyes were wild. "Is there hope in this King?"

"He is dark," hissed the Gruagach with a wild shake of its shaggy head, and its eyes rolled aside and fixed again on his. "O dark."

"Who? What meaning, dark? Name me names. Will this young King live?"

The Gruagach gave a moan and suddenly bit him fiercely, so that he jerked his hand back and lost the Gruagach from his grip, holding the wounded hand to his lips. But the creature stopped and hugged itself and rocked to and fro, wild eyed, and spoke in a thin, wailing voice:

Dark the blight and dark the path and strong the chains that bind them

Fell the day that on them dawns, for doom comes swift behind them.

"What sense is that?" Niall cried. "Who are *they*? Do you mean myself?"

"No, no, never Cearbhallain. O Man, the Gruagach weeps for you."

"Shall I die then?"

"All Men die."

"A plague on you!" He sucked at his wounded hand. "What chains and where? Is it Caer Wiell you mean?"

"Stay," it said, and fled.

He almost had the will to go. He stood on the hillside and looked down at the dale that led away toward the outgoing of the hills. But that *Stay* rang in his ears, and his bones ached with his running, and Caoimhin was nowhere in sight.

He sank down there, and watched till sundown, but the courage for the road grew colder and colder, and his belief in it less and less.

At last a boy came running, jogging along by turns and running as if his side hurt, down in the place between the hills.

"Scaga!" Niall called, rising to his feet.

The boy stopped as if struck, and looked up, and began to run toward him, stumbling as he ran; but Niall came down to him and caught him in his arms.

"I thought you had gone," the boy said, and never Scaga wept, but his lip quivered.

"Caoimhin is gone," Niall said, "not I. Is supper ready?"

For a moment Scaga fought for breath. "I think so."

So he came back with Scaga, and the snare was fast.

FOUR

The Hunting

Arafel dreamed. It was only a moment of a dream, a slipping elsewhere into memory, which she did much, into a brightness much different from the dim nights and blinding days and mortal Eald. But her time being never what the time of Men was, she had hardly time to sink to sleep again when a sound had waked her, a plaintive sound and strange.

He has come back again, she thought drowsily, no little annoyed; and then she sought and found something quite different—a fell thing had gotten in, or came close, and something bright fled ringing through her memory.

She gathered herself. The dream scattered in pieces beyond recall, but she never heeded. The wind blew a sound to her and all of Eald quivered like a spider web. She took a sword and flung her cloak about her, though she could have done more. It was carelessness and habit; it was fey ill luck, perhaps. But no one challenged Arafel; so she followed what she heard.

There was a path through Eald, up from the Caerbourne ford. It was the darkest of all ways to be taking out of Caerdale, and since she had barred it few had traveled it: brigands like the outlaw—this kind of Man might try it, the sort with eyes so dull and dead they were numb to ordinary fear and sense. Sometimes they were even fortunate and won through, if they came by day, if they moved quickly and never tarried or hunted the beasts of Eald. If they sped quickly enough then evening might see them safe away into the New Forest in the hills, or out of Eald again to cross the river.

But a runner entering by night, and this one young and wild-eyed and carrying no sword or bow, but only a dagger and a harp—this was a far rarer venturer in Eald, and all the deeper shadows chuckled and whispered in their startlement.

It was the harp she had heard, this unlikely thing which jangled on his shoulder and betrayed him to all with ears to hear, in this world and the other. She marked his flight by that sound and walked straight into the way to meet him, out of the soft cool light of the elvish sun and into the colder white of his moonlight. Unhooded she came, the cloak carelessly flung

THE GRUAGACH

back; and shadows which had grown quite bold in the Ealdwood of latter earth suddenly felt the warm breath of spring and drew aside, slinking into dark places where neither moon nor sun cast light.

"Boy," she whispered.

He started in mid-step like a wounded deer, hesitated, searching out the voice in the brambles. She stepped full into his light and felt the dank wind of mortal Eald on her face. The boy seemed more solid then, ragged and torn by thorns in his headlong flight through the wood. His clothes were better suited to some sheltered hall—they were fine wool and embroidered linen, soiled now and rent; and the harp at his shoulders had a broidered case.

She had taken little with her out of otherwhere, and yet did take: it was always in the eye which saw her. She had come as plainly as ever she had ventured into the mortal world, and leaned against the rotting trunk of a dying tree and folded her arms without a hint of threat, laying no hand now to the silver sword she wore. More, she propped one foot against a projecting root and offered him her thinnest smile, much out of the habit of smiling at all. The boy looked at her with no less apprehension for that effort, seeing, perhaps, a ragged vagabond in outlaw's habit—or perhaps seeing more and having more reason to fear, because he did not look to be as blind as some. His hand touched a talisman at his breast and she, smiling still, touched that pale green stone which hung at her own throat, a talisman which had power to answer his.

"Now where would you be going," she asked him, "so recklessly through the Ealdwood? To some misdeed? Some mischief?"

"Misfortune, most like." He was out of breath. He still stared at her as if he thought her no more than moonbeams, which amused her in a distant, dreaming way. She took in all of him, the fine ruined clothes, the harp on his shoulder, so very strange a traveler on any path in all the world. She was intrigued by him as no doings of Men had yet interested her; she longed—But suddenly and far away the wind carried a baying of hounds. The boy cried out and fled away from her, breaking branches in his flight.

His quickness amazed her out of her long indolence, catching her quite by surprise, which nothing had done in long ages. "Stay!" she cried, and stepped into his path a second time, shadow-shifting through the dark and the undergrowth like some trick of moonlight. She had felt that other, darker presence; she had not forgotten, far from forgotten it, but she was light with that threat, having far more interest in this visitor than any other. He touched something forgotten in her, brought something of brightness in himself, amid the dark. "I do doubt," she said quite casually to

THE GRUAGACH

calm him, the while he stared at her as if his reason had fled him, "I do much doubt they'll come this far. What is your name, boy?"

He was instantly wary of that question, staring at her with that trapped deer's look, surely knowing the power of names to bind.

"Come," she said reasonably. "You disturb the peace here, you trespass my forest—What name do you give me for it?"

Perhaps he would not have given his true one and perhaps he would not have stayed at all, but that she fixed him sternly with her eyes and he stammered out: "Fionn."

"Fionn." *Fair* was apt, for he was very fair for humankind, with tangled pale hair and the first down of beard. It was a true name, holding much of him, and his heart was in his eyes. "Fionn." She spoke it a third time softly, like a charm. "Fionn. Are you hunted, then?"

"Aye," he said.

"By Men, is it?"

"Aye," he said still softer.

"To what purpose do they hunt you?"

He said nothing, but she reckoned well enough for herself.

"Come then," she said, "come, walk with me. I think I should be seeing to this intrusion before others do.—Come, come, have no dread of me."

She parted the brambles for him. A last moment he delayed, then did as she asked and walked after her, carefully and much loath,

retracing the path on which he had fled, held
by nothing but his name.

She stayed by that track for a little distance,
taking mortal time for his sake, not walking
the quicker ways through her own Eald. But
soon she left that easiest path, finding others.
The thicket which degenerated from the dark
heart of Eald was an unlovely place, for the
Ealdwood had once been better than it was,
and there was still a ruined fairness about
that wood; but these young trees they began to
meet had never been other than desolate. They
twisted and tangled their roots among the bones
of the crumbling hills, making deceiving and
thorny barriers. It was unlikely that any Man
could ever have seen the ways she found, let
alone track her through the night against her
will—but she patiently made a way for the boy
who followed her, and now and again waiting,
holding branches parted for him. So she took
time to look about her as she went, amazed
by the changes the years had wrought in this
place she once had known. She saw the slow
work of root and branch and ice and sun, labored hard-breathing, mortal-wise, and scratched
with thorns, but strangely gloried in it, alive
to the world this unexpected night, waking
more and more. Ever and again she turned
when she sensed faltering behind her: the boy
each time caught that look of hers and came
on with a fresh effort, pale and fearful as he
seemed, past clinging thickets and over stones;

doggedly, as if he had lost all will or hope of doing otherwise.

"I shall not leave you alone," she said. "Take your time."

But he never answered, not one word.

At last the woods gave them a little clear space, at the veriest edge of the New Forest. She knew very well where she was. The baying of hounds came echoing up to her out of Caerdale, from the deep valley the river cut below the heights, and below was the land of Men, with all their doings, good and ill. She thought a moment of her outlaw, of a night he sped away; a moment her thoughts ranged far and darted over all the land; and back again to this place, this time, the boy.

She stepped up onto the shelf of rock at the head of that last slope, while at her feet stretched all the great vale of the Caerbourne, a dark, tree-filled void beneath the moon. A towered heap of stones had lately risen across the vale on the hill. Men called it Caer Wiell, but that was not its true name. Men forgot, and threw down old stones and raised new. So much did the years do with the world.

And only a moment ago a man had sped—or how many years?

Behind her the boy arrived, panting and struggling through the undergrowth, and dropped down to sit on the edge of that slanting stone, the harp on his shoulders echoing. His head sank on his folded arms and he wiped the sweat and the tangled pale hair from his brow. The baying, which had been still a moment, began again much nearer, and he lifted frightened eyes and clenched his hands on the rock.

Now, now he would run, having come as far as her light wish could bring him. Fear shattered the spell. He started to his feet. She leapt down and stayed him yet again with a touch of light fingers on his sweating arm.

"Here's the limit of my woods," she said, "and in it hounds do hunt that you could never shake from your heels, no. You'd do well to stay here by me, Fionn, indeed you would. Is it yours, that harp?"

He nodded, distracted by the hounds. His eyes turned away from her, toward that dark gulf of trees.

"Will you play for me?" she asked. She had desired this from the beginning, from the first she had felt the ringing of the harp; and the desire of it burned far more keenly than did any curiosity about Men and dogs—but one would serve the other. It was elvish curiosity; it was simplicity; it was, elvish-wise, the truest thing, and mattered most.

The boy looked back into her steady gaze as though he thought her mad; but perhaps he had given over fear, or hope, or reason. Something of all three left his eyes, and he sat down

THE GRUAGACH

on the edge of the stone again, took the harp
from his shoulders and stripped off the case.

Dark wood starred and banded with gold, it
was very, very fine: there was more than mortal skill in that workmanship, and more than
beauty in its tone. It sounded like a living
voice when he took it into his arms. He held it
close to him like something protected, and lifted
a pale, still sullen face.

Then he bowed his head and played as she
had bidden him, soft touches at the strings
that quickly grew bolder, that waked echoes
out of the depths of Caerdale and set the hounds
in the distance to baying madly. The music
drowned the voices, filled the air, filled her
heart, and now she felt no faltering or tremor
of his hands. She listened, and almost forgot
which moon shone down on them, for it had
been long, so very long, since the last song had
been heard in the Ealdwood, and that was sung
soft and elsewhere.

He surely sensed a glamor on him, in which
the wind blew warmer and the trees sighed
with listening. The fear passed from his eyes,
and while the sweat stood on his face like
jewels, it was clear, brave music that he made.

Then suddenly, with a bright ripple of the
strings, the music became a defiant song,
strange to her ears.

Discord crept in, the hounds' fell voices which
took the music and warped it out of tune. Arafel
rose as that sound grew near. The harper's

hands fell abruptly still. There was the rush and clatter of horses in the thicket below.

Fionn himself sprang to his feet, the harp laid aside. He snatched at once at the small dagger at his belt, and Arafel flinched at the drawing of that blade, the swift, bitter taint of iron. "No," she wished him, wished him very strongly, and stayed his hand. Unwillingly he slid the weapon back into its sheath.

Then the hounds and the riders came pouring up at them out of the darkness of the trees, a flood of dogs black and slavering and two great horses clattering among them, bearing Men with the smell of iron about them, Men glittering terribly in the moonlight. The hounds surged up the slope baying and bugling and as suddenly fell back again, making a wide circle, alternately whining and cringing and lifting their hackles at what they saw. The riders whipped them, but their horses shied and screamed under the spurs and neither horses nor hounds could be driven farther.

Arafel stood, one foot braced against the rock, and regarded this chaos of Men and beasts with cold curiosity. She found them strange, harder and wilder than the outlaws she knew; and strange too was the device on them, a wolf's grinning head. She did not recall that emblem—or care for the manner of these visitors, less even than the outlaws.

A third rider came rattling up the slope, a

THE GRUAGACH

large man who gave a great shout and whipped
his unwilling horse farther than the other two,
all the way to the crest of the hill facing the
rock, and halfway up that slope advanced more
Men who had followed him, no few of them
with bows. The rider reined aside, out of the
way. His arm lifted. The bows bent, at the
harper and at her.

"Hold," said Arafel.

The Man's arm did not fall: it slowly lowered.
He glared at her, and she stepped lightly up
onto the rock so that she need not look up so
far, to this Man on his tall black horse. The
beast suddenly shied under him and he spurred
it and curbed it cruelly; but he gave no order
to his men, as if the cowering hounds and
trembling horses had finally made him see what
he faced.

"Away from there!" he shouted at her, a voice
fit to make the earth quake. "Away! or I dare-
say you need a lesson too." And he drew his
great sword and held it toward her, curbing
the protesting horse.

"Me, lessons?" Arafel stepped lightly to the
ground and set her hand on the harper's arm.
"Is it on his account you set foot here and raise
this noise?"

"My harper," the lord said, "and a *thief.*
Witch, step aside. Fire and iron can answer
the likes of you."

Now in truth she had no liking for the sword
the Man wielded or for the iron-headed arrows

yonder which could come speeding their way
at this Man's lightest word. She kept her hand
on Fionn's arm nonetheless, seeing well enough
how he would fare with them alone. "But he's
mine, lord-of-Men. I should say that the harper's
no joy to you, or you'd not come chasing him
from your land. And great joy he is to me,
for long and long it is since I've met so pleasant
a companion in the Ealdwood—Gather the harp,
lad, do, and walk away now. Let me talk to
this rash Man."

"Stay!" the lord shouted; but Fionn snatched
the harp into his arms and edged away.

An arrow hissed: the boy flung himself aside
with a terrible clangor of the harp, and lost the
harp on the slope. He might have fled, but he
scrambled back for it and that was his undoing.
Of a sudden there was a halfring of arrows
drawn ready and aimed at them both.

"Do not," said Arafel plainly to the lord.

"What's mine is *mine*." The lord held his
horse still, his sword outstretched before his
archers, bating the signal. "Harp and harper
are *mine*. And you'll rue it if you think any
words of yours weigh with me. I'll have him
and *you* for your impudence."

It seemed wisest then to walk away, and
Arafel did so. But she turned back again in the
next instant, at distance, at Fionn's side, and
only half under his moon. "I ask your Name,
lord-of-Men, if you aren't fearful of my curse."

So she mocked him, to make him afraid be-

THE GRUAGACH

fore his men. "Evald of Caer Wiell," he said back in spite of what he had seen, no hesitating, with all contempt for her. "And yours, witch?"

"Call me what you like, lord." Never in human ages had she showed herself for what she was, but her anger rose. "And take warning, that these woods are not for human hunting and your harper is not yours anymore. Go away and be grateful. Men have Caerdale. If it does not plase you, shape it until it does. The Ealdwood's not for trespass."

The lord gnawed at his mustaches and gripped his sword the tighter, but about him the drawn bows had begun to sag and the loosened arrows to aim at the dirt. Fear was in the bowmen's eyes, and the riders who had come first and farthest up the slope hung back, free men and less constrained than the archers.

"You have what's mine," the lord insisted, though his horse fought to be away.

"And so I do. Go on, Fionn. Do go, quietly."

"You've what's *mine*," the valley lord shouted. "Are you thief then, as well as witch? You owe me a price for it."

She drew in a sharp breath and yet did not waver in or out of the shadow. It was so, if his claim was true. "Then do not name too high, lord-of-Men. I may hear you, if that will quit us. And likewise I will warn you: things of Eald are always in Eald. Wisest of all if what you ask is my leave to go."

His eyes roved harshly about her, full of

hate and yet a weariness as well. Arafel felt cold at that look, especially where it centered, above her heart, and her hand stole to that moon-green stone which hung uncloaked at her throat.

"I take leave of no witch," said the lord. "This land is mine—and for my leave to go— the stone will be enough," he said. *"That."*

"I have told you," she said. "You are not wise."

The Man showed no sign of yielding. So she drew it off, and still held it dangling on its chain, insubstantial as she was at present—for she had the measure of them and it was small. "Go, Fionn," she bade the harper; and when he lingered yet: *"Go!"* she shouted. At the last he ran, fled, raced away like a mad thing, clutching the harp to him.

And when the woods all about were still again, hushed but for the shifting and stamp of the horses on the stones and the whining complaint of the hounds, she let fall the stone. "Be paid," she said, and walked away.

She heard the hooves racing at her back and turned to face treachery, fading even then, felt Evald's insubstantial sword like a stab of ice into her heart. She recoiled elsewhere, bowed with the pain of it that took her breath away.

In time she could stand again, and had taken from the iron no lasting hurt. Yet it had been close: she had stepped otherwhere only narrowly in time, and the feeling of cold lingered even in the warm winds. She cast about her, found the clearing empty of Men and beasts, only trampled bracken marking the place. So he had gone with his prize.

And the boy—She went striding through the shades and shadows in greatest anxiety until she had found him, where he huddled hurt and lost in a thicket deep in Eald.

"Are you well?" she asked lightly, concealing all concern. She dropped to her heels beside him. For a moment she feared he might be hurt more than the scratches she saw, so tightly he was bowed over the harp; but he lifted his pale face to her in shock, seeing her so noiselessly by him. "You will stay while you wish," she said, out of a solitude so long it spanned the age of the trees about them, of a stillness so deep the leaves of them never moved. "You will harp for me." And when he still looked at her in fear: "You'd not like the New Forest. They've no ear for harpers there."

Perhaps she was too sudden with him. Perhaps it wanted time. Perhaps Men had truly forgotten what she was. But his look achieved a perilous sanity, a will to trust.

"Perhaps not," he said.

"Then you will stay here, and be welcome. It is a rare offer. Believe me that it is."

"What is your name, lady?"

"What do you see of me? Am I fair?"

Fionn looked swiftly at the ground, so that

she reckoned he could not say the truth without offending her. And she mustered a laugh at that in the darkness.

"Then call me Feochadan," she said. "*Thistle* is one of my names and has its truth—for rough I am, and have my sting. I'm afraid it's very much the truth you see of me.—But you'll stay. You'll harp for me." This last she spoke full of earnestness.

"Yes." He hugged the harp closer. "But I'll not go with you, understand, any farther than this. Please don't ask. I've no wish to find the years passed in a night and all the world grown old."

"Ah." She leaned back, crouching near him with her arms about her knees. "Then you *do* know me.—But what harm could it do you for years to pass? What do you care for this age of yours? The times hardly seem kind to you. I should think you would be glad to see them pass."

"I am a Man," he said ever so quietly. "I serve my King. And it's *my* age, isn't it?"

It was so. She could never force him. One entered otherwhere only by wishing it. He did not wish, and that was the end of it. More, she sensed about him and in his heart a deep bitterness, the taint of iron.

She might still have fled away, deserting him in his stubbornness. She had given a price beyond all counting and yet there was retreat and some recovery, even if she spent human

THE GRUAGACH

years in waiting. In the harper she sensed
disaster. He offended her hopes. She sensed
mortality and dread and all too much of human-
ness.

But she settled in the sinking moonlight,
and watched beside him, choosing instead to
stay. He leaned against the side of an aged
tree, gazed at her and watched her watching
him, eyes darting to the least movement in the
leaves, and back again to her, who was the
focus of all ancientness in the wood, or dangers
to more than life. And at last for all his cau-
tion his eyes began to dim, and the whispers
had power over him, the sibilance of leaves
and the warmth of dreaming Eald.

FIVE

The Hunter

Fionn slept, and waked at last by sunrise, blinking and looking about him in plain fear that trees might have grown and died of old age while he slept. His eyes fixed on Arafel last of all and she laughed in elvish humor, which was gentle if sometimes cruel. She knew her own look by daylight, which was indeed as rough as the weed she had named herself. She seemed tanned and thin and hard-handed, her gray-and-green all cobweb patchwork, and only the sword stayed true. She sat plaiting her hair in a single silver braid and smiling sidelong at the harper, who gave her back a sidelong and anxious glance.

All the earth had grown warm in that morning. The sun did come here, unclouded on this day. Fionn rubbed the sleep from his eyes and opening his wallet, began looking for his breakfast.

There seemed very little in it: he shook out a bit of jerky, looked at it ruefully, then split off a bit of it with his knife and offered half his breakfast to her—so small a morsel that, halved, was not enough for a Man, and a haggard and hungry one at that.

"No." she said. She had been offended at once by the smell of it, having no appetite for man-taint, or the flesh of any poor forest creature. But the offering of it, the desperate courtesy, had thawed her heart. She brought out food of her own store, a gift of trees and bees and whatsoever things felt no hurt at sharing. She gave him a share, and he took it with a desperate dread and hunger.

"It's good," he pronounced quickly and laughed a little, and finished it all. He licked the very last from his fingers, and now there was relief in his eyes, of hunger, of fear, of so many burdens. He gave a great sigh and she smiled a warmer smile than she was wont, remembrance of a brighter world.

"Play for me," she wished him.

He played for her then, idly and softly, heart-healing songs, and slept again, for bright day in Ealdwood counseled sleep, when the sun burned its warmth through the tangled branches and brambles and the air hung still, nothing breathing, least of all the wind. Arafel drowsed too, at peace in mortal Eald for the first time since many a tree had grown. The touch of the mortal sun did that kindness for her, a benison she had all but forgotten.

But as she slept she dreamed, and there were halls in that vision, of cold gray stone.

In that dark dream she had a Man's body, heavy and reeking of wine and ugly memories, such a dark fierceness she would gladly have fled it running if she might. She felt the hate, she felt the weight of human frame, the reeling unsteadiness of strong drink.

He had had an unwilling wife, had Evald of Caer Wiell—Meara of Dun na h-Eoin was her name; he had a small son who huddled afraid and away from him in the upstairs of this great stone keep, the while Evald drank with his sullen kinsmen and cursed the day. Evald brooded and he hated, and looked oftentimes at the empty pegs on his wall where the harp had hung. The song gnawed at him, and the shame gnawed at him, bitter as the song—for that harp came from Dun na h-Eoin, as Meara came.

Treason, it had sung once, and the murder of kings and bards. Keeping it was his victory.

So Evald sat and drank his ale and heard the echoes of that harping. And in her dream Arafel's hand sought the moonstone on its chain and found it at his throat.

She had laid a virtue on it in giving it, that he could neither lose it nor destroy it. Now she

THE GRUAGACH

offered him better dreams and more kindly as he nodded, for it had that power. She would have given him peace and mended all that was awry in him, drawing him back and back to Eald. But he made bitter mock of any kindness, hating all that he did not comprehend.

"No," whispered Arafel, grieving, dreaming still before that fire in Caer Wiell. She would have made the hand put the stone off that foul neck; but she had no power against the virtue she herself had given it, so far, so wrapped in humankind, while *he* would not. And Evald possessed what he owned, so fiercely and with such jealousy it cramped the muscles and stifled the breath.

Most of all he hated what he did not have and could not have; and the heart of it was the harper and the respect of those about him and his lust for Dun na h-Eoin.

So she had erred, and knew it. She tried to reason within this strange, closed mind. It was impossible. The heart was almost without love, and what little it had ever been given it folded in upon itself lest what it possessed escape.

He had betrayed his King, murdered his kinsmen, and sat in a stolen hall with a wife who despised him. These were the truths which gnawed at him in his darkness, in the stone mass which was Caer Wiell.

Of these he dreamed, and clenched the stone tightly in his fist, and would never let it go:

this was all he understood of power—to hold, and not let go.

"Why?" asked Arafel of Fionn that night, when the moon shed light on the Ealdwood and the land was quiet, no ill thing near them, no cloud above them. "Why does he seek you?" Her dreams had told her Evald's truth, but she sensed another in the harper.

Fionn shrugged, his young eyes for a moment aged; and he gathered his harp against him. "This," he said

"You said it was yours. He called you thief. What then did you steal?"

"It is mine." He settled it in his arms, touched the strings and brought forth melody. "It hung in his hall so long he thought it was his, and the strings were cut and dead."

"And how did it come to him?"

Fionn rippled out a somber note and his face grew darker. "It was my father's and his father's before him, and they harped in Dun na h-Eoin before the Kings. It is old, this harp."

"Ah," she said, "yes, it is old, and one made it who knew his craft. A harp for kings. But how did it come to Evald's keeping?"

The fair head bowed over the harp and his hands coaxed sound from it, answerless.

"I've given a price," she said, "to keep him from it and from you. Will you not give back an answer?"

The sound burst into softness. "It was my

THE GRUAGACH

father's. Evald hanged him in Dun na h-Eoin, in the court when it burned. Because of songs my father made, for truth he sang, how men the King trusted were not what they seemed. Evald was the least of that company, not great; petty even in that great a wrong. When the King died, when Dun na h-Eoin was burning, my father harped them one last song. But he fell into their hands and so to Evald's—dead or living, I never knew. Evald hanged him from the tree in the court and took the harp of Dun na h-Eoin for his own. He hung it on his own wall in Caer Wiell for mock of my father and the King. So it was never his."

"A king's own harper."

Fionn never looked at her and never ceased to play. "Ah, worse things he has done. But that was seven years ago. And so I came, when I was grown—wandering the roads and harping in all the halls. Last of all to Caer Wiell. Last of all to him. All this winter I gave Evald songs he liked. But at winter's end I came down to the hall at night and mended the old harp. So I fled over the walls. From the hill I gave it voice and a song he remembered. For that he hunts me. And beyond that there is no more to tell."

Then softly Fionn sang, of humankind and wolves, and that song was bitter. Arafel shuddered to hear it, and quickly bade him cease, for mind to mind with her in troubled dreams

Evald heard and tossed, and waked starting in sweat.

"Sing more kindly now," she said. "More kindly. It was never made for hate, this harp, this gift of my folk to the Kings of Men. There were such gifts once long and long ago, did you not know? It sounds through all the realms of Eald, mine and thine and places far darker. Never sing dark songs. Harp me brighter things. Sing me sun and moon and laughing, sing me the lightest song you know."

"I know children's songs," he said doubtfully. "Or walking songs. The great songs—well, it seems an age for dark ones."

"Then sing the little ones," she said, "the small ones that make Men laugh—oh, I have need to laugh, harper, that most of all."

Fionn did so, while the moon climbed above the trees, and Arafel recalled elder-day songs which the world had not heard in long years, sang them sweetly. Fionn listened and caught up the words in his strings, until the tears ran down his face for joy.

There could be no harm in Ealdwood in that hour: the spirits of latter earth which skulked and strove and haunted Men fled elsewhere, finding nothing in this place that they knew; and the old shadows slipped away trembling, for they remembered.

But now and again the elvish song faltered, for there came a touch of ill and smallness into

THE GRUAGACH

Arafel's own mind, a cold piercing as the iron,
bringing thoughts of hate, which she had never
held so close.

Then she laughed, breaking the spell, and
put it from her. She bent herself to teach the
harper songs which she herself had almost
forgotten, conscious the while that elsewhere,
down in Caerbourne vale, on the hill of Caer
Wiell, a Man's body tossed in sweaty dreams
which seemed constantly to mock him, with
sounds of eldritch harping that stirred echoes
and sleeping ghosts.

With the dawn, she and Fionn rose and
walked a time, and shared food, and drank at a
cold, clear spring she knew, until the sun's hot
eye fell upon them and cast its numbing spell
on all the Ealdwood.

Then Fionn slept in innocence, while Arafel
fought the sleep which came to her. Dreams
were in that sleep, her time to dream while *he*
should wake, Evald, the lord in the valley, and
those dreams would not stay at bay, not as her
eyes grew heavy and the midmorning air thickened with urging sleep. They pressed at her
more and more strongly. The Man's strong legs
bestrode a great brute horse, and his hands
plied the whip and his feet the spurs, hurting
it cruelly. She dreamed the noise of hounds
and hunt, a coursing of woods and hedges and
the bright spurt of blood on dappled hide—Evald
sought blood to wipe out blood, because the

harping still rang in his mind, and he remembered ... harper, and hall, and the harper who had sung the truth of how he served his king. He hunted deer and thought other things. She shuddered at the killing her own hands did, and at the fear that gathered thickly about the valley lord, reflected in his comrades' eyes, reflected in his wife's and son's pale faces when he came riding home again with deer's blood on his clothes.

It was better that night, when the waking was Arafel's and her harper's, and sweet songs banished fear and dreams. But even then Arafel recalled and grieved, and at times the cold came so heavily on her that her hand would steal to her throat where the moongreen stone had hung. Her eyes brimmed once suddenly with tears. Fionn saw that, and tried to sing her merry songs instead.

They failed, and the music died.

"Teach me another song," he begged of her, attempting distraction. "No harper ever had such songs. And will *you* not play for *me?*"

"I have no art," she said, for the last true harper of her own folk had gone long ago to the sea. The answer was not all truth. Once she had played. But there was no more music in her hands, none since the last of her folk had gone and she had willed to stay, loving this woods too well in spite of Men. "Play," she asked of Fionn, and tried desperately to smile, though the iron closed about her heart and the valley lord raged at the nightmare, waking in sweat, ghost-ridden.

It was that human song which Fionn had played in his despair on the hillside, bright and defiant that it was: Eald rang with it; and that night the lord Evald did not sleep again, but sat shivering and wrapped in furs before his hearth, his hand clenched in hate on the stone which he possessed and would not, though it killed him, let go.

But Arafel quietly began to sing, a song of elder earth unheard since the world had dimmed. The harper took up the tune, which sang of earth and shores and water, the last great journey, at Men's coming and the changing of the world. Fionn wept while he played, and Arafel smiled sadly and at last fell silent, for it was the last of all elvish songs. Her heart had gone gray and cold.

The sun returned at last, but Arafel had no will now to eat or rest, only to sit grieving, because she had lost her peace. She would have been glad now to have fled the shadow-shifting way back into otherwhere, to her own fair moon and softer sunlight. She might have persuaded the harper to come with her now. She thought now perhaps he could find the way. But now there was a portion of her heart in pawn, and she could not even take herself away from this world: she was too heavily bound to thoughts of it. She fell to mourning and despair, and often pressed her hand where the stone should rest. It was time, the shadows whispered, that Eald should end. She held in ancient stubbornness And she felt some feyness on her, that many things together had gone amiss, that even on her the harp had power

He hunted again, did Evald of Caer Wiell, now that the sun was up. Sleepless, driven mad by dreams, he whipped his folk out of the hold as he did his hounds, out to the margin of the Ealdwood, to harry the creatures of the woods' edge—having guessed well the source of his luck and the harping in his dreams. He brought fire and axes across the Caerbourne's dark flood, meaning to fell the old trees one by one until all was dead and bare.

The wood muttered now with whisperings and angers. A wall of cloud rolled down from the north on Ealdwood and all deep Caerdale, dimming the sun. A wind sighed in the faces of the Men, so that no torch was set to wood for fear of fire turning back on the hold itself; but axes rang, all the same, that day and the next. The clouds gathered thicker and the winds blew colder, making the Ealdwood dim again and dank. Arafel still managed to smile by night, hearing the harper's songs. But every stroke of the axes by day made her shudder, and while Fionn slept by snatches, the iron about her heart grew constantly closer. The wound in the

Ealdwood grew day by day, and the valley lord was coming: she knew it well.

And at last there remained no rest at all, by day or night

She sat then with her head bowed beneath the clouded moon, and Fionn was powerless to cheer her. He sat and regarded her with deep despair, and reached and touched her hand for comfort.

She said no word to that offering, but rose and invited the harper to walk with her awhile. He did so. And vile things stirred and muttered in the shadow of the thickets and the briers, whispering malice to the winds, so that often Fionn started aside and stared and kept close beside her.

Her strength was fading, first that she could not keep these voices away, and then that she could not keep herself from listening. *Ruin,* they whispered. *All useless.* And at last she sank on Fionn's arm, eased to the cold ground and leaned her head against the bark of a gnarled and dying tree.

"What ails?" he asked, and patted her face and pried at her clenched and empty fingers, opened the fist which hovered near her throat, as if seeking there the answer. "What ails you?"

She shrugged and smiled and shuddered, because even now by the glare of fires and torches in the dark, the axes had begun again, and she felt the iron like a wound, a great cry going through the wood as it had gone ceaselessly for days; but he was deaf to it, being what he was.

"Make a song for me," she said.

"I have no heart for it."

"Nor have I," she said. A sweat stood on her face, and he wiped at it with his gentle hand and tried to ease her pain

And again he caught and unclenched the hand which rested, empty, at her throat. "The stone," he said. "Is it *that* you miss?"

She shrugged, and turned her head, for the axes then seemed loud and near. He looked that way too—and glanced back deaf and puzzled, to gaze into her eyes

" 'Tis time," she said. "You have to be on your way this morning, as soon as there's sun enough. The New Forest will hide you after all."

"And leave you? Is that what you mean?"

She smiled, touched his anxious face. "I'm paid enough."

"How paid? What did you pay? *What* was it you gave away?"

"Dreams," she said. "Only that. And all of that." Her hands shook terribly, and a blackness came on her heart too miserable to bear: it was hate, and aimed at him and at herself and all that lived; and it was harder and harder to fend away. "Evil has it. He would do you hurt, and I would dream that too. Harper, it's time to go."

"Why would you give such a thing?" Great

tears started from his eyes. "Was it worth such a cost, my harping?"

"Why, well worth it," she said, and managed such a laugh as she had left to laugh, that shattered all the evil for a moment and left her clean. "I have remembered how to sing."

He snatched up the harp and ran, breaking branches and tearing flesh in his headlong haste, but not, she realized in horror, not the way he ought—but back again, to Caerdale.

She cried out her dismay and seized at branches to pull herself to her feet; she could in no wise follow. Her limbs which had been quick to run beneath this moon or the other were leaden, and her breath came hard. Brambles caught and held with all but mindful malice, and dark things which had never had power in her presence whispered loudly now, of murder.

And elsewhere the wolf-lord with his men drove at the forest with great ringing blows, the poison of iron. The heavy human body which she sometime wore seemed hers again, and the moonstone was prisoned near a heart that beat with hate.

She tried the more to make haste, and could not. She looked helplessly through Evald's narrow eyes and saw—saw the young harper break through the thickets near them. Weapons lifted, bows and axes. Hounds bayed and lunged at leashes in the firelight.

Fionn came, nothing hesitating, bringing the harp, and himself. "A trade," she heard him say. "The stone for the harp."

There was such hate in Evald's heart, and such fear, it was hard to breathe. She felt a pain to the depth of her as Evald's coarse fingers pawed at the stone. She felt his fear, felt his loathing of the stone. Nothing would he truly let go. But this—this, he abhorred, and was fierce in his joy to lose it.

"Come," the lord Evald said, and held the stone dangling and spinning before him, so that for that moment the hate was far and cold.

Another hand took it then, and very gentle it was, and very full of love. She felt the sudden draught of strength and desperation—she sprang up then, to run, to save—

But pain stabbed through her heart, with one last ringing of the harp, with such an ebbing out of love and grief that she cried aloud, and stumbled, blind, dead in that part of her.

She did not cease to run; and she ran now that shadow-way, for the heaviness was gone. Across meadows, under that other light she sped, and gathered up all that she had left behind, burst out again in the blink of an eye and elsewhere

Horses shied in the dark dawning and dogs barked; for now she did not care to be what suited men's eyes. Bright as the moon she broke among them, and in her hand was a sharp silver sword, to meet with iron.

Harp and harper lay together, sword-riven. She saw the underlings start away from her and cared nothing for them; but Evald she sought, lifted that fragile silver blade. Evald cursed at her, drove spurs into his horse and rode down at her, sword swinging, shivering the winds with a horrid sweep of iron. The horse screamed and shied; he cursed and reined the beast, and drove it for her again. But this time the blow was hers, a scratch that made him shriek with rage.

She fled at once. He pursued. It was his nature that he must. She might have fled elsewhere and deceived him, but she would not. She darted and dodged ahead of the great horse, and it broke down the brush and the thorns and panted after, hard-ridden.

Shadows gathered, stirring and urgent on this side and on that, who gibbered and rejoiced for the way the chase was tending, to the woods' blackest heart—for some of them had been Men; and some had known the wolf's justice, and had come by that to what they were. They reached, these shadows, but durst not touch him: she would not have it so. Over all the trees bowed and groaned in the winds and the leaves went flying as clouds took back the dawn in storm: thunder in the heavens and thunder of hooves below, cracks of brush scattering the shadows.

Suddenly in the dark of a hollow she whirled, flung back her dimming cloak and the light gleamed suddenly: the horse shied up and fell, casting Evald sprawling among the wet leaves. The shaken beast scrambled up and evaded its master's reaching hands and his threats, thundered away on the moist earth, breaking branches as it went, splashing across some hidden stream in the dark, and then the shadows chuckled. Arafel stood still, fully in his world, moonbright and silver. Evald cursed, shifted that great black sword of his in his hand, which bore a scratch now that must trouble him. He shrieked with hate and slashed.

She laughed and stepped into otherwhere as iron passed where she had stood, shifted back again and fled yet farther, letting him pursue until he stumbled with exhaustion and sobbed and fell in the storm-dark forgetting now his anger, for the whispers came loud, in the moving of the trees.

"Up," she bade him, mocking, and stepped again to *here*. Thunder rolled above them on the wind, and the sound of horses and hounds came at distance.

Evald heard the sounds. A joyous malice came into his eyes at the thought of allies; his face grinned in the lightnings as he gathered his sword.

She laughed too, elvish-cruel, as the horses

neared them—and Evald's confident mirth died as the sound came over them, shattering the heavens, shaking the earth—a Hunt of a different kind, from a third and other Eald.

Evald cursed and swung the blade, lunged and slashed again, and she flinched from the almost-kiss of iron. Again he whirled his great sword, pressing close. She stepped elsewhere, avoiding the iron, stepped back again with her silver blade set full in his heart and suddenly *here*. The lightning cracked—he shrieked a curse, and, silver-spitted—died.

She did not weep or laugh now; she had known this Man too well for either. She looked up instead to the clouds, gray wrack scudding before the storm, where other hunters coursed the winds and wild cries wailed across belated dawn—heard hounds baying after something fugitive and wild. She lifted then her fragile sword, salute to lord Death, who had governance over Men, a Huntsman too; and many the old comrades the wolf would find following in *his* train.

Then the sorrow came on her, and she walked the otherwhere path to the beginning and end of her course, where harp and harper lay, deserted, the Wolf's comrades all fled. There was no mending here. The light was gone from his eyes and the wood of the harp was shattered.

But in his fingers lay another thing, which gleamed like the summer moon in his hand.

Clean it was from his keeping, and loved. She gathered the moonstone to her. The silver chain went again about her neck and the stone rested where it ought. She bent last of all and kissed him to his long sleep, fading then to otherwhere.

And the storm grew.

S I X

Setting Forth

The storm had come over the Steading, a wall of cloud and wind which whipped the branches of the oak and ripped the young spring leaves.

And in it Caoimhin came home, running breathless, panting and stumbling as he came along the fence row, fighting the wind which drove across his path.

So he came to the gate and up the path, and young Eadwulf who had come out to see the sheep saw him first: "Caoimhin!" Eadwulf cried.

But Caoimhin passed on, running and holding his side. Blood was on his face. Eadwulf saw that and clambered over the pen and ran after him

So Niall saw him, not knowing him at first, seeing only that a man had come to the Steading: he left his securing of the barn against the

storm and came running from the other side as
many did from many points of the Steading,
from the house and from the pens, leaving
their work in haste.

But when he had come into Caoimhin's way
his heart turned in him, seeing the quiver and
the bow, the gauntness of the man, the recent
scar that crossed his unshaven face, the blood
that ran on it from scratches.

"Caoimhin!" Niall said and caught him up
arm to arm. "Caoimhin!"

Caoimhin fell, collapsing to his knees, and
Niall went down to his own, holding his arms
while Caoimhin's body heaved with his breathing. The bloody face lifted again, glazed with
sweat, pale and gaunt. His beard and hair
showed dirt and grass from his falling. "Lord,"
Caoimhin said, "he's dead, Evald is lost and
dead."

A moment Niall stared at him blankly and
Caoimhin's hands gripped his arms as the others gathered round. "Dead," Niall said, but nothing else he understood. "But you are back,
Caoimhin—You found the way."

"*Dead,* hear me, Cearbhallain." Caoimhin
found strength to shake at him. "Caer Wiell is
without a lord—it is your hour, your hour, Cearbhallain. He went into the wood and never out
again; he has crossed the fair folk and never
will he come out again. Fionn—"

"Is he with you?"

"The harper's dead. Evald killed him."

THE GRUAGACH

"Coinneach's son."

"*Listen to me*. There is no time but now. There are men would ride with you, I have told you—"

"The harper dead."

"Cearbhallain, are you deaf to me?" The tears poured down Caoimhin's face. *"I came back for you."*

Niall knelt still in the dust. Beorc was there, and set his large hands on Caoimhin's shoulders. Most of the Steading gathered and was still gathering, some standing, some kneeling near, and the latest come were shushed so the silence thickened, a deep and terrible waiting.

"Tell me," Niall said, "when and where. Tell me from the beginning."

"From time to time—" Caoimhin caught his breath, leaning his hands now on his knees. "We met, Coinneach's son and I. Fionn Fionnbharr. On the road, when I went after him. And so we parted. Only he brought word to me now and again—how he fared, and where. He wintered in Caer Wiell as he had said he would and the men—I have gathered old friends, my lord, men you knew. I have never been idle, about the roads and the hills and the fringes of the river; I have been to Donn and Ban and all such places and back again, and sent men to Caer Luel—"

"—in my name?"

"What less would bring them? Aye, your name. But we have kept quiet, lord, and hunted and done little—in your name. And we took our news from the harper when he could bring it, even from Caer Wiell. But lately he fled the hold—fled with Evald behind him, and so they report him dead, murdered—but Evald himself died after, this very morning. A man of ours was hidden near his camp; and brings word his men believe him dead—fear other things less lucky to talk of—in this storm—" Caoimhin fought for breath and caught his arms. "They will be riding back to Caer Wiell this morning, today, lordless, and leaderless—Caer Wiell is yours again. You cannot deny it now. Men are ready to follow you—Fearghal and Cadawg and Dryw, Ogan, the lot of them—"

"You had no right!" Niall flung Caoimhin's hands aside and rose, swung his arm to clear himself a space and stopped at the shocked and staring faces of those about him, of Lonn and the others, and turned back to look on Beorc himself, his eyes stinging in the wind which howled and whipped about them. Lastly he looked down at Caoimhin, who looked up at him, hurt and worn as the world had worn him, bearing such scars as he had been spared in the Steading, where no war could come—and all at once his peace was shattered beyond recall. It was not a clap of thunder, although thunder rolled; it was only a sudden clear sight, how men fared that he once had loved, how life and death had gone on for all the world without him. He felt robbed, for in the stormlight

THE GRUAGACH

everything about him seemed dimmed and less beautiful than it had been. There was gray about the Steading, which had never been. There were flaws in the faces about him he had never seen. Tears started from his eyes and ran crooked in the wind. "So, well, we ought to be on our way," he said, and helped Caoimhin to his feet. It was hard to look at the others, but he must, at Beorc's solemn face, whose red mane whipped in the gale; at Aelfraeda, whose golden braids were immovable in strongest winds; at Siolta and Lonn, steadfast; at Scaga whose thin young face had hollowed almost to manhood in the passing years. "I have a thing to see to," Niall said to them. "Like for the wolf and foxes—there comes a time, doesn't there? The deer are gone. They'll hunt one another in the hills."

"You'll want food," said Aelfraeda.

"If you will," Niall whispered and looked at Beorc. "If you will—Banain—"

"She will bear you," said Beorc, "I do not doubt. And if she will, then what she wills."

"I need my sword," Niall said then, and turned away, not having the heart for facing Beorc or Aelfraeda any longer. He flung his arm about Caoimhin. "Come up to the house. There'll be ale and bread at least."

So they went. He found Scaga at his left, trudging along with him and Caoimhin, and so he set his left hand on Scaga's shoulder, but the boy bowed his head and said nothing to him, nothing at all, while the thunder rumbled over the Steading and the wind blew the young leaves of the oak in shreds.

They came into the house, into warmth and a busy flurrying after drink and bread and the wherewithal to feed two and more hungry men on their way. Niall went to the corner by the fire and took his sword, but he did not draw it, not even to see to the blade of it. The sheath and hilt were covered with dust. Perhaps rust had gotten to it as it lay by the hearth. But it was not a thing for bringing to light in Beorc's house and in Aelfraeda's. Diarmaid brought the remnant of the armor he had had, and this he put on with Scaga and Lonn and Diarmaid to help him, while Caoimhin sat shaking with weariness and cramming food into his mouth. He had no cloak any longer. He put on the warm vest he had had on before, hung the dusty sword on his shoulder and went out into the chill of the storm to find Banain in the barn.

"I'll come with you," Scaga cried after him, following him outside.

"No," he shouted back to the porch. "Stay warm. Help Aelfraeda. I'll not be leaving without seeing you. Stay inside."

The thunder cracked. He turned and ran, past the gate of the yard and down the hill to the barn and so inside, where was shelter from

THE GRUAGACH

the wind and the warm smell of straw and horses

"Banain," he whispered, coming to her in the shadow of the stall. He brought the bridle she had been wearing when she came to them. They had mended its broken rein for the children's riding; but he had never put it on her. He hugged her about the neck and got a nudging in the ribs in return, a whickering from the pony near her in the dark. "Banain," he said. "Banain."

"Cruel," a small voice piped

He whirled about with his back to the mare. The Gruagach sat on the pony's back, peering at him across the rails of the next stall.

"Cruel to take Banain. Cruel Caoimhin, to take his lord away. O where is peace, Man? Never, never, for Caoimhin; now never for Banain; never for Cearbhallain. O never go."

"I would I never had to." He recovered himself and turned about again, stroking Banain's neck. His hands were still cold from the wind outside. He coaxed the bit into Banain's mouth and drew the strap past her ears. She turned her head and butted him gently in the chest, snorted as a dark shape landed on the rail in front of them.

"Never go," said the Gruagach.

"I have no choice."

"Always, always comes a choice. O Man, the

Gruagach warns you." It shifted and hugged itself upon its rail. "Wicked Caoimhin, wicked."

Niall took the cheekstrap and backed Banain out of her warm nest of straw and comfort. The Gruagach followed, a scurrying in the straw: it came out into the light of the half-open door well-dusted, with straws in its hair, and hugged itself and rocked. "Never go," it said

A sadness came on Niall. He would never have expected such a feeling toward the Gruagach, but he knew that where he fared would be nothing like the creature, never in all the cold strange world. Already it seemed small and wizened and more afraid than frightening. He held out his hand as he would have to a child. "Gruagach," he said, "take care of the people I love. And this place. I have stayed too long."

The Gruagach touched his hand with fingertips, so, so lightly, and cocked his head and looked up at him, then shivered and bounded away to the top of the apple-bin, burying his head in his arms. "She sees, she sees," he wept, "o the terrible face, the terrible lights of her eyes, she sees!"

"Who?" asked Niall. "What—sees?"

"She was waked," the Gruagach cried, looking from between his arms. "She is waked, waked, waked! and the harp of Kings is broken. O the terrible sword, the sharp, the wicked sword! O never go, Man, O Man, the Gruagach warns you never go."

THE GRUAGACH

"Who is *she?*"

"In the forest, deep and still. The harp came there because it had to come. Things of Eald must. Beware, o beware of Donn."

The thunder rumbled and muttered over them. Banain threw her head. "I have no choice," Niall said shivering. "I never had. Farewell."

He flung open the door and led Banain out. He would have shut it for the pony's sake, but the Gruagach was in the doorway. He swung up to Banain's back and rode up toward the house, from which the others were coming down.

So he should not have the chance to come into the house again. He felt cheated—of even that little time. The world seemed the colder as the wind howled and whipped at him and Banain, who danced and fretted under him for distaste of this weather and for the thunder—and never yet it rained. Something keened. It was not the wind. He looked up and behind him and saw the Gruagach perched on the rooftop of the barn, a lumpish knot of hair.

"Man," it wailed. "O Man."

The others came about him, Caoimhin and Beorc and Aelfraeda and all the house so far as he could judge. "Here," said Niall, flinging a leg over Banain's back. "Caoimhin, you must ride. You're spent."

Caoimhin would not, not without arguing about it; but Niall slid down and put him up, and on his own shoulders he took the healthy

pack Aelfraeda had put up for them. He kissed
her cheek and pressed Beorc's hand. He looked
round on all the faces, and they seemed already far from him, slipping away from him, a
love he did not know how to hold onto any
longer.

"Scaga," he said, missing one. "Where is
Scaga?"

Everyone looked around, but the boy was
not to be found. "He was with me," said Siolta,
"only a moment ago. "

"He is hurt," said Lonn.

So Niall shook his head heavily, well under-
standing that. "Come," he said to Caoimhin,
and hitched the cords of the pack on his
shoulder. "Good-bye," he said. "Good-bye."

"Fare well," said Beorc, "and wisely. A blessing beyond that I cannot give you, though I
would."

Niall turned his shoulder then and walked
beside Caoimhin on Banain. The wind battered
at them, and never a drop of rain fell from the
black clouds above. The grass and the tender
crops flattened in waves, and now and again
the lightning flashed in the clouds. He looked
back more than once and waved each time, but
now they all seemed hazy, shadowed under the
storm that had come over the Steading. His
heart felt heavier and heavier and his steps
were leaden.

"Have care," a small voice wailed from the
hilltop at his right. "Have care." It was the

THE GRUAGACH

Gruagach, sitting on a stone in a sea of blowing grass. "O Man, it is no common rain this brings."

"That fell creature," Caoimhin muttered.

"Speak it fair," said Niall. "O Caoimhin, speak it only fair."

But it was gone, the rock deserted. Banain tossed her head and snorted in the wind.

"Here, lord, she can carry two," Caoimhin said. "Ride with me."

"No," said Niall. A last time he looked back, but a hill was passing between him and those behind: he waved a last time, but they perhaps did not see. He felt a loneliness and desolation, blinked as some wind-borne dust hit his eyes and rubbed at them as he walked along, blind for the moment. When he had gotten them clear he looked back again, squinting in the gusts.

The fences at least should have been in sight. There was only the blowing grass. "Caoimhin," he said, "the fences are gone."

Caoimhin looked, but never said a word. Again Niall rubbed his eyes, feeling a great cold settle into his bones, as if the wind had finally gotten through. Caoimhin had found his way back again, the thought came to him; Caoimhin had come as the harper had come, never reckoning how hard it was—for need, for need of *him*. A haste had come on him, all the same, a blind numb haste to go back to the world again: Ogan, Caoimhin had named the

names—Ogan and Dryw and the others, names
that he had known, bloody names of bloody
years, of *his* years with the King—

And Caer Wiell, to go home again, to whatever home was left—

"Niall!" he heard cry from the hill above
him, a human, cracking voice, wind-thinned.
"Caoimhin! Niall!"

"Scaga," Niall said, and his heart turned
over in him. "Scaga, no."

But the boy came running—boy: he was near
a man. He came down the hill and joined them,
panting as if his ribs would crack, for he had
come the longer, harder way.

"Go back," Niall said, shaking him by the
arms.

"I will follow," Scaga said reasonably, "lord."

Niall flung his arms about him; there was
nothing left to do. Caoimhin had gotten down
off Banain and hugged him too.

So they went, down among the hills, Caoimhin
riding mostly and they two jogging along beside,
then taking turn about.

"By the river we will find them," Caoimhin
said. "There."

SEVEN

Meara

Women grieved in Caer Wiell, a slow sort of
grief, lacking substance or hope. The hunters
came home by evening without their quarry
and without their lord—men scratched and torn
and haunted by long wandering in the wood.
They drank together now in the hall, a silent,
brooding crowd, whose eyes kept much to the
table and to their ale. One man wept, his head
bowed into his arms. He was the only one.

In her upstairs chamber Meara sat with her
arm about her small son and the boy leaning
his dark head against her skirts—not asleep,
but drowsing sometimes in his weariness and
his fright. Meara sat still and silent, so that
the maid, the only servant left her, dared not
move or question anything.

"They brought neither home," Meara said at last when the boy had drifted off. She looked toward the tall slit window, toward the night and still-brooding storm. "And they do not come upstairs. So they are not yet sure that he is dead." She stroked her son's drowsing head, looked toward young Cadhla the maid, who had pretended to be at sewing and left it now in her lap. There was stark, constant fear in Cadhla's eyes. There was no law in Caer Wiell this night but fear. The thunder that had rumbled all the day, unnatural, cracked and shook the ancient stones. Then the rain began, at long last, a natural, driving rain. Cadhla looked toward the ceiling, a great and shaken sigh as if some long-held breath had passed her lips as if all nature had been holding its breath. The boy lifted his head. "Hush," said Meara, "It's only rain."

"Does he come?" the boy asked.

"Hush, no, be still. Shall I hold you?"

He reached. Meara took him up. He was a lad of five and mostly too proud to be held, but she took him into her lap and rocked him now.

"Lady," said Cadhla, "let me."

"No," said Meara, just that: "No." So Cadhla stayed, and, looking down, pricked at ill-made stitches, flinching from the thunderclaps. The rain sluiced down the walls, a constant spatter and whisper, and the trees sighed down by the Caerbourne's flood. Ever and again a gust whipped at the curtains and sent the lamps and candles flickering, but the child slept on. From the hall came a clattering of metal, but quiet fell again below, leaving only the rain

"They do not come," the lady Meara said again in the softest of voices, only for Cadhla's ears. "But tomorrow if he has not come home again, then they will come upstairs."

"Lady," whispered Cadhla, "what shall **we** do?"

"Why, I go to the strongest," the lady Meara said, "as I did before." She looked down at her sleeping son. Her hand smoothed his dark cap of hair. His small fist clenched the tighter on her sleeve. He was never a hearty child, Evald's son, but small and quick to understand too much. "Hush, what can we do? What could we ever do? But if you can you must be away with him, you understand?"

"Aye," said Cadhla softly, her blue eyes round. "I will." But both of them understood the chances of it, Meara most of all. Gently she caressed her sleeping son, well knowing the men downstairs, that one of them would soon take ambition; and then there was no chance for the boy, no chance at all for any bearer of Evald's blood to survive—perhaps not even past the dawn. There were Beorhthramm and the others, fell and bloody men, wild and bloody as her lord ... and growing more drunken with every passing hour. The cups were filled again and again downstairs; and cowards gathered the courage they had lost in the woods.

But distant, from outside the window in the dark, from beneath the walls, came the hoofbeats of a running horse.

Meara lifted her head and listened through the thunder and the rush of wind and rain.

"Off the road," whispered Cadhla. "It comes from under the walls, not the gate."

It grew nearer still, seemed to rush beneath the window, and echoed off the stone, distinct in spite of the water's rushing and the blowing of the leaves. A moment it lingered below, then seemed to move on again, and the thunder muttered.

"O lady," Cadhla breathed, clutching the luckpiece at her throat, "it be faery, that."

"It would be my husband's horse come home," said Meara, and her eyes were far and cold. "But it could circle the hold all night and they will not unbar the gates to see, no, they are haunted men. Hush," she said, for the boy stirred in his sleep, and she rocked him, hugged him. The hoofbeats came back again and lingered.

"Faery," Cadhla insisted when the pacing went on and on. "O lady—"

But the hoofbeats passed away into the dark, and below, in the hall, no door was opened or closed: no one went out to see. So the sound died, and the hall grew quiet in the abating of the rain. There were not even footsteps below.

THE GRUAGACH

The child slept exhausted in Meara's arms, and Cadhla stopped her shivering. The curtain flapped; it had come undone in the wind which now had sunk away. Meara waved a hand toward it and with dread Cadhla got up and approached the dark window to tie it fast, then began to trim the lamps one by one, a homely act and peaceful in a hall that waited murder.

"You'll sleep a bit," Cadhla said when she had done. She offered her shawl. With a gesture Meara bade her spread it so, over the boy, and some peace they had after that. Cadhla fell asleep in the chair they had set against the door, her hands fallen in her lap, her head resting on her ample breast.

But Meara kept her watch, and listened to the rain which had mostly spent its fury. No tears fell from her eyes, not now. They are for yesterday, she thought to herself, and for tomorrow. Had the window been wide enough she would have thought of escape; of braiding together all the cloth they had and so letting themselves down. But it was far too narrow for any but her son. She thought desperately of waiting until those below were sunk in their cups and so trying to run with him, passing through that hall. But there was the watch below to pass, and they might be less drunken.

Perhaps, perhaps, she thought, she could win time for her son, only a little time; and wise Cadhla, faithful Cadhla might find a way for him and her, a country woman and not so lost as she. Or Cadhla might somehow get outside the gates and she might let down her son to Cadhla's arms.

Or perhaps, after all, her lord would come home—he was safety, at least, from worse than himself. And this was the hope which turned her coward, for from the tower there was no way to escape but the hall below and the drunken men.

She might feign a mourning for her lord; but any of them who knew her would laugh at that; nor respect it even if it were true.

They might fight among themselves, that being the way of them when they had no one to stop them; and that was all the respite she could hope for, perhaps a day to save her son. But that contest only the bloodiest of them would win.

A door opened in the dark, far away and muffled. Meara heard, and shivered in the long cold, near the dawn, waking from almost-sleep with her son's weight leaden in her arms. He comes home, she thought without thinking. He has come to the gates after all, bloody and angry.

But she doubted that. She doubted every hope of safety except Cadhla still sleeping against the door. She looked down at her son's face. That wayward lock of hair had strayed again onto his cheek. She dared not move to brush it away, fearing to wake him. Let him sleep, she

thought, o let him sleep. He will be less afraid
if he can sleep.

She heard steps of more than one man coming up from the wardroom below, as one came
into the hall. So, she thought with a chill up
her back, it *is* himself; he has come up with
the gatekeeper, or waked someone below. We
are safe, we are safe if only we stay still—for
she knew in her heart of hearts that if the
ruffians had left their lord horseless and alive
in the forest, then there would be a grim
reckoning for that.

Then came a ring of steel, and a cry—a clatter of metal and the dying screams of men.

"Ah!" cried Meara and hugged her frightened son to her breast. "Hush, no, be still, be
still."

"It would be himself," sobbed Cadhla, bolt
upright, her hands before her lips. "Oh, he has
come back!"

In a moment the cries and the blows and the
screaming became loud. The boy shivered in
Meara's arms, and Cadhla ran to them and
hugged them both and shivered along with
them.

"It is not," said Meara then, hearing the
voices, and turned cold at the heart. Someone
was coming up the stairs in haste. "O Cadhla,
the door!"

The latch was down but that was never stout
enough. Cadhla flung herself for that chair
before the door to add her weight to it, but the

door crashed open before her and flung the chair against the wall. Men red with blood stood there, with swords naked in their hands.

Cadhla stopped still between, making herself a barrier.

But one came last through the door, a long-faced man in a shepherd's coat and carrying a sword, undistinguished by any badge or arms, but marked by a quiet uncommon in Caer Wiell. His hair was long and mostly grayed, his lean face seamed with scars. A grim, wide-shouldered man came in at his back, and last, a red-haired youth with a cut across his brow.

"Lady Meara," the invader said. "Call off your defender."

"Cadhla," Meara said. Cadhla came aside and stood against the wall, her busy eyes traveling over all the men, her small mouth clamped tight. There was a dagger beneath her apron and her hand was not in sight.

But the tall stranger came as far as Meara's feet and sank down on one knee, the bloody sword clasped in the crook of his arm.

"Cearbhallain," Meara said half doubting, for the face was aged and changed

"Meara Ceannard's daughter. You are widowed, if that is any grief to you."

"I do not know," she said. Her heart was beating fast. "You must tell me that."

"This is my hold. My cousin is dead—and not at my hand, though I will not say as much

THE GRUAGACH

for men of his below. Caer Wiell is in my hands."

"So are we all," she said. It was all before her, the hope of passing the gates in safety, the hopelessness of wandering after. "I may have kin in Ban."

"Ban swings with every wind. And what then for you—the wolf's widow? Seek shelter of An Beag? The wolf's friends are not trustworthy. Caer Wiell is *mine,* I say; and I will hold it." He put out his hand to the boy, whose fists were clenched tight in Meara's sleeve, who flinched from the stranger's touch. "Is he yours?"

Never yet the tears had fallen. Meara held them now, while this large and bloody hand stretched out toward her son, her babe. "He is mine," she said. "Evald is his name. But he is *mine.*"

The hand lingered a moment and left him. "Evald's heir has nothing from me; but I will treat him as a son and his mother—if she stays in Caer Wiell—will be safe while I can make her so."

With that he rose and gave a sign to his men, only some of whom remained. "Guard this door," he bade them. "Let no one trouble them. They are innocent." He looked down again, a grim figure still, and holding the bloody sword still in his arm, for it could not be sheathed. "If my cousin should come home again he will have a bitter welcome. But I do not expect he will."

"No,' said Meara, and shivered. For the first time the tears fell. "There would be no luck for him now."

"There was no luck for him in Caer Wiell while he had it," said Niall Cearbhallain. "But I will hold it, by my own."

She bowed her head and wept, that being all there was to do. "Mother," her son wailed; she held him close for comfort, and Cadhla came and held them too.

"I would not come down to the hall," said Cearbhallain, "until we have cleansed it." And he went away, never smiling, never once smiling. But Meara laughed, laughed as she had almost forgotten how.

"Free," she said. "Free!—o Cadhla, he is Niall Caerbhallain, the King's own champion! O cleansed the hall! That they have, they have. I knew him once—oh, years and years ago; and the morning has come and our night is over."

A furtive hope had burst in Meara's eyes, a shielded, suspecting hope, as every hope in Caer Wiell was long apt to be twisted and used for hurt. It forgot that the young harper Fionn was dead and lost; forgot an almost-love, for she was still young and the harper had touched her heart in her desolation. She forgot, forgot, and set all her future hopes on Cearbhallain. That was the nature of the niece of the former King, who had learned how to live in storms, that she knew how to find another staying place.

THE GRUAGACH

"Mother," her son said—he said little always, did Evald's son: he had learned his safety too, small that he was, which was silence, to clench his small fists on what help there was and never to let go. "Is he coming?"

"Never," she said, "never again, little son. That man will keep us safe."

"There was blood on him."

"It was the blood of all the wicked in Caer Wiell. But he would never hurt us."

So she rocked her son, and the strength left her of a sudden, so that Cadhla must catch them both. And still Meara laughed.

There was a marriage made in Caer Wiell, when the warmth of summer came. There were new faces in the hold, stark, grim men, but soft-spoken and courteous, and no few of them Meara had known in her youth, who smiled to see her, those of them who remembered to smile at all. Some folk remained from the Caer Wiell that was, but the worst had died or fled and the rest had mended what they were; and more and more came to the gates, even farmers who hoped for land—which they got as long as there was land fallow. There were some kinsmen of Niall's, but few; there was a motley lot of folk met over the hills and in them, wild sorts and never to be crossed. There was Caoimhin, lame from the attack; and gangling Scaga; and grim, mad lord Dryw from the southern hills. But whatever the nature of them, there was law, and more, word spread abroad in what ill-luck the wolf had died, which kept the mutterings from An Beag and Caer Damh only mutterings: they had no desire to trifle with the wood and the power in it. They had felt the storm. So they were content to close the road and to pen Caer Wiell in its remoteness—as if there were anywhere to go.

So Meara wed, decked in flowers and quiet as she was always quiet, and became Niall's lady in Caer Wiell.

And the boy Evald dogged Niall's steps and Caoimhin's and Scaga's; and learned play and laughter.

"He is your son," Niall would say to Meara, which he knew pleased her. "And my cousin, and the blood of the Kings is in him on your side."

But at times he saw another thing, when the boy was crossed, when his temper rose. And then twice as resolutely Niall used patience with young Evald, for there were times when the boy could melt his heart, when he laughed or when, though tired, he tried to follow, matching a grown man's steps. He would go everywhere with Niall, onto the walls, up the stairs and down, into the stables and storerooms. A word from Niall could light his eyes or cloud them, and there was no stopping such adoration.

So the boy grew, and if at times Scaga cuffed his ears when he needed it, Evald no more than frowned; it was only Niall could get tears

THE GRUAGACH

from him. He had a pony to ride, a shaggy beast rescued from the mill, and it thrived and became a merry wicked kind of pony, jogging along by Banain on summer rides. Evald outgrew all his clothes by winter, and all his sleeves were let out, and his waists likewise, keeping Cadhla busy. And on winter nights he listened to the warriors' tales.

But never to anything of Eald, for at any such tale Meara drew him to herself and shivered, so in this Niall forbore

Meara bore a daughter for him, a fair blue-eyed child; and after her a sister, so he had no son, but this was, if a matter to him, still no real grief—for his luck had brought him two, Scaga, who went to broad-shouldered manhood, a dour young man who managed well the sometime defense against An Beag; who learned his soldiery of men who had fought the long hard war; and he had Evald, who grew to youth— his heir, for Scaga had no thought of ruling anything. As for Evald, Evald was innocent in his assumption that the hold was his ... for he was fierce and prideful in his devotion—and learned to be gentle too, giving all his heart to those who gave to him—for so Niall had taught him.

So Niall had his daughters and loved them wholeheartedly, and they inherited Evald's pony when he had outgrown it. To Evald he gave Banain's latest foal instead.

Caoimhin died, the greatest grief that came

to Niall in those happy years: it was a simple
fall, his lame leg betraying him on the stairs.
So Caoimhin slept in the heart of Caer Wiell,
of a kind of death he had never looked to die, a
peaceful one

The trees grew again across the river. Snow
fell and melted into spring, and Caer Wiell
began a new tower—for, said Niall, one never
knew what the times would bring. Mostly in
his heart was the thought of the King, who
was now toward his manhood, and that wars
might come which he would never see—for age
was coming on him. His hair had gone from
grey to white, and one day he sent Banain
away, for she was failing and he could no longer
pretend the years away. He sent Scaga to lead
her, and a troop of his armed men, as if the
piebald mare had been some great chieftain
under escort, for they had to pass the road that
An Beag held: and so they did, with never a
stirring from An Beag, which chose to watch
more of late than act, having learned bitter
lessons.

So Banain went, free up the dell.

"She ran," Scaga reported later, his eyes
alight. "She seemed doubtful a moment, and
then she threw her head and lifted her tail and
ran the way she could when she was young. I
lost sight of her; the hills came between. But
she knew the way. I do not doubt it."

"You might have followed her yourself," Niall
said, and the tears shimmered in his eyes.

THE GRUAGACH

"So might you," said Scaga. "I have my wife, my son—my home here."

"Well, well, and Banain is home. " He set his lips. "So, well, but so am I, and so are you, that's true. That's true. There's a time to let things go even when we love them."

"Lord," said Scaga, his strong face now much concerned. "You are out of heart about the mare. You were right. It was her time, but it's not yet yours."

"Caoimhin is gone. Of all the rest he had no ties; would I could have sent him."

"He would never have left you."

"Would never have left Caer Wiell," Niall said. "It was the land he loved, these stones; and now he sleeps in the heart of them. I have Meara and Evald and my daughters—That foal of Banain's will serve me, but a strongwilled horse she is. I never liked her half so well."

"We will hunt tomorrow, lord, and change you mood."

"I never found much joy in it, I tell you truth. It minds me of things."

"Then we will ride and let the deer do as they like."

"So. Yes," said Niall, and gazed into the embers from his chair before the fire. A stone wolf's head was above the hearth. It stared back at him. He had never taken it away.

EIGHT

The Luck of Niall Cearbhallain

The seasons passed. For long, for very long
there was peace—for the young King was a
rumor in the hills, and if men spoke well of
him, still his day was not yet dawned. So traitors aged who had had most guilt; and true
men grew old as well.

"You must do what I cannot," Niall would
say to Evald of the King; and poured his hopes
into him and taught him arms. "He is your
cousin," Niall would say. "And you will set
him on his throne. As I would."

Any war in which Niall would not be foremost seemed very far to Evald, for out of his
childhood this man had come, already gray,
and soon white-haired, but vigorous, a storm
that scoured out the hold and scoured the land of
every injustice he could find; and rode at times,

he or his men, to remind his enemies whose hand ruled in Caerdale. And Evald, who remembered only hurt before this man came and took him to his heart, had never thought those days would end. But end they did, at first without his realizing it—for first Caoimhin went, and then Banain, and Dryw went back to his mountains, and then Scaga took most of the border-riding on himself, while Niall sat at home. And so age came on him. So it came to a small talk in the hall, not the first such sober talk, but the deepest.

"Time will come," said Niall, "when I am gone; and men will talk—mark you, son, I love you. But true it is you are my son by love and not by blood. The King's own cousin: never you forget it. But Evald's too; you are my cousin and not my son. There are those faithful who will stand by you come what may: you know their names. But men will whisper and try to bring you down, that being the way of men."

"Then I will fight them," said Evald. "And you will not be gone. Never speak of it."

"That would not be wise." Niall reached for a pitcher and poured wine into his cup, poured another for him. "So. I have a match for you in mind."

The color fled Evald's face and flooded it. He took the cup. He was sixteen and until that moment he had been a boy, thought like one, mostly for the hunt and games and dreams of

glory in the skirmishes with An Beag; but he
shared a cup with his father, rare honor, and
asked quietly: "Who?"

"Dryw's daughter."

"Dryw!"

"His daughter, I say, not the man."

"Dryw is—"

"Not the cheeriest of men that were my
friends. But the youngest and well-gifted with
sons—a fierce lot. He has one daughter, dear
to his heart. His sons have one sister. And
they care for their own. I could set no truer
folk at your back than Dryw's. It would ease
my mind."

"Because the man who sired me was one
who killed the king." Evald lowered his head.
He had never said as much, but he had heard.

"Because you are my heir," Niall said sternly.
Then more gently: "I would not see the alliances I made slip away from you. Dryw I trust;
his sons I would trust if you had a bond to
them. Her name is Meredydd."

"What does Mother say?"

"That is the wisest thing to do."

"What says lord Dryw?"

"He is yet to ask. First I ask my son."

"So, well," Evald said uncomfortably. "Yes.
If it's right." It was unfair. There was nothing
Niall could not have asked of him. For love of
Niall and his mother he would have flung him-
self on spears, this being the direst kind of fate
he had imagined for himself, warriorlike to

THE GRUAGACH

keep Caer Wiell. He had never thought that
there were other ways. This dismayed him more
than enemies, that he had to suddenly become
a man in many ways, and to be wise, and to
get children of his own.

"This year," said Niall.

"So soon."

"I don't count my time in years."

"Sir—"

" 'Twould please me and please your mother.
I think of her. I would see you with the strongest allies I can find—for her sake, if I am
gone."

"She will always be safe."

"Of course she will." Niall drank and put on
a merrier face, and smiled for him, which was
always like a stone that had learned to smile,
so lean and hard he was.

But looking at him Evald grew afraid, perceiving for the first time that he was, after all,
old; and that his riding out of the hold was
growing hard for him, and his limbs were not so
strong as they had been. So Banain had begun,
growing thinner, bonier in the knees, until she
stopped being young, and they took her to the
hills. Evald believed no fables: Banain was
dead; his pony had died this spring leaving
his sisters heartbroken, and he cherished no
illusions.

Why must things die at all? he thought. Or
grow old? And he thought with terror that the
curse was on him too, that now he must be a

man and learn to trade in councils what men
traded, and that fighting for the King when he
should rise might be something less glorious
and more the slow and lifelong battle it had
been for Niall.

Evald's son, they would call him, and never
trust him without the claim of his mother's
blood and Cearbhallain's allies to support him.
He lost his boyhood in that thinking, and knew
what, somewhere in the depth of his heart, he
had always feared: that he might lose Cearbhallain himself and slip back into the dark from
which Cearbhallain had rescued him. They sang
songs of Cearbhallain, of bloody Aescford, of
bravery and wit and gallant deeds; and this
man fostered him and shielded him and his
mother, which he was old enough to understand was not the least of the gallantries of
Cearbhallain. He remembered the harper, if
very dimly, a golden vision and bright songs;
he remembered mostly pain of his true father,
blood and pain and a harsh loud voice; and one
night of shining metal and hands with the
blood of all those who had ever hurt his mother.
She had laughed that night, and ever after
smiled, and Niall had let no more blood come
near her—he washed when he had come home
from fighting on the border and never would
see them until he and all the men with him
had put off their armor and all the manner of
war—because this is Caer Wiell, Niall said,

THE GRUAGACH

not a robber hold like An Beag. And so the men about him learned to say.

But that was years ago. Before the tower rose.

It is for me, Evald thought, full of dread, and looked up at the scaffolding and the jagged stone against the sky. He builds it for me, not for himself. And then the foreboding came on him that it was the last thing Niall might do.

I do not reckon my time in years, he had said.

So month by month of summer the tower rose toward its roofing, and in all those months Niall rode but seldom, and ached much of nights: Meara tended him gently in his sometime illness, and Evald saw how the gray had touched her hair as well, and how worn she grew as his father failed. Only Niall smiled and won her smile from her. But most times Meara wore a worried look.

Month by month the messengers went back and forth with Dryw; and that grim man came, all grayed himself, a lean clamp-jawed man with young men about him who looked little more than thieves—his sons. "So, well," Dryw said having looked Evald up and down, "I have had my spies. They report well of the boy."

"My father speaks well of you," Evald said, which impertinence brought the mountain lord's cold eye back to him and gained a frown.

"Which father?" Dryw asked with Niall there to witness.

"The one who calls you friend," Evald said sharply, "and whose opinions of men I honor." —Which pleased Dryw and made him laugh his dry chill laugh and clap Niall on the arm.

"He is not easily at a loss," said Dryw. And so they sent him away and arranged particulars together, Dryw and Niall, like two farmers chaffering over sheep.

So it was done, and Niall reckoned he had done the best he could. Spring, Dryw promised; Meredydd should come by spring. So Dryw and his sons went home again before the winter snows and Evald walked about with that stricken, panicked look about him that he had had that day of the talk in the hall—but it was well done, well done, Niall told himself, and so Meara said—For, said Meara, now he has kin of mine on the one side and friends of yours on the other.

"And he has Scaga," Niall said. "He has Scaga, truest and closest," which eased his heart to think on.

But that, with his tower, seemed enough. It seemed too wearying to bundle into heavy garments and go riding in the autumn chill; the fire was comfort. Many things which he had done of duty he left now to younger hands, and while he thought it would be splendid, as the snow fell, to saddle up and ride, to hear the hooves crunching the snow, the steady whuff of breath, and to feel the keen edge of the wind

THE GRUAGACH

against his face—it would not be Banain under him. And to wrap up to take a ride to exercise some horse his men could do as much for seemed pointless, when his men must shelter him from any hostile meeting, when the most that they might look for was a cup of cheer at some farmhouse—but that put him all too keenly in mind of other things he missed. So he forever thought he would like to do these things, and the wanting was joy enough, not to be spoiled by doing. The best thing was his fireside, and listening to the harper who had come to his hall (but nothing like Fionn Fionnbharr, so even that joy paled). At last there was the fire's warmth against the cold that crept into his limbs, and good food, and Meara's kindness and his folk about him. He was fading, that was all, a gentle fading, so that he went all to gauntness.

"I shall see the spring," he said to Meara. "That long I shall live." What he meant was that he should see his son wed, but that seemed too grim a promise set against a wedding: and Meara shook her head and shed tears over him, scolding at him finally, which well contented him: so he smiled to please her. In all he was very tired, and thought the winter would be enough for him. His dreams when he dreamed were of that place between the hills; of orchards bare with winter; of walking knee-deep in snow to the barn and of the smell of bread when he was coming home.

He became a burden: he feared he was. He lay about much in the hall. His son and his daughters cared for him—for his daughters too he intended marriages, young as they were, and sent messages, and arranged one for Ban and his youngest for one of Dryw's grim sons, the best that he could do. So even in his fading his reach was far, and he took care for years to come. But Meara surprised him in her devotion and her tears—a deep surprise, for it had never semed love on her part, only habit; for his part it was tenderness, a habit, too. It was the only thing which grieved him, that he had always been scattered here and there, doing this or that for her, and for the children, and never knowing that very simple thing.

Had he loved her, he wondered? He was not sure whether he had loved anything as it deserved, only he had done his duty by everything, save only a little while, a few years for himself, to which his mind kept drifting back for refuge. But he had been very fortunate, he thought, that his duty had brought so much of love to him.

And he had made a place for gentler things. That, most. He had brought a little of the Steading with him. It all seemed a dream, and that of Aescford dimmest, and Dun na h-Eoin, and the very walls of Caer Wiell. What was real was a fire, a fish, a shadow among the oaks; but—strange—he was not afraid this time.

THE GRUAGACH

And a small brown face with eyes like murky water.

O Man, it said, O Man—come back.

Niall Cearbhallain was dying. There was no longer any hiding it. An Beag had made trial of the borders, but prematurely: Scaga drove them out again, and harried them within sight of their own hold for good measure, before grief and concern drew him back again. So Scaga was there by the hall both day and night, and had armed men stationed here and there about the countryside; and farmers to light watchfires if anything stirred.

It was all, Evald recognized, well done, as Niall himself would have ordered it—as perhaps Niall had ordered it in his clearer moments, to the man who was his right hand and much of his heart.

So Dryw came, winter as it still was, and the frosts still too bitter for any greening of the land. He came riding up the Caerbourne with enough armed men about him to force his way if he must, like a cold wind out of the southern heights—so unlooked for that at first the outposts took alarm. But then they could see his banners from the walls, the blue and the white, and the first cheer came that Caer Wiell had known for days

Evald watched them ride beneath the gates. It was, he knew, like what his father had told him of Dryw, not to waste time with messengers, and for the first time he felt an affection for that skull-faced madman. They came with rattle of armor and the gleam of spears and expected to be housed; but among them came a pony with ribbons in its mane, and on that pony rode a cloak-shrouded girl.

"Meredydd," he whispered, slinking from the wall as if he had seen something best forgot. He had no heart for marryings. Not now, never now.

But, "Yes," his father said when Dryw had come to him. "Yes, good for you, old friend." His mind was clear, at least this evening.

So Evald met his bride, who was a thin girl whose clothes ill-fit her, and whose eyes looked nervously over him. Meara had scarcely any time for her with so much on her thoughts, so Evald was left to murmur courtesies in the lesser hall. He was only grateful she had brought her nurse to take care of her.

"I wish," Meredydd said mouselike, from the door in leaving to go upstairs, "I wish I had got my best dress finished. It doesn't fit."

This was all very far from him, but he saw the red in her cheeks and saw how young she was. "It was good of you to come sooner than you promised," he said. "That was more important."

Meredydd lifted her face and looked at him, seeming heartened.

She was not, he decided, what he had planned, but not what he had dreaded either, having a

THE GRUAGACH

capable way about her when she looked like
that. And truth, she quickly had her own bag-
gage up the stairs and ordered her own room
and was down seeing to her father's housing
and running back and forth with this and that,
taking loads from the servants and sending
them on other errands so deftly all that number was fed, while his mother took the respite
offered her and simply stayed by his father's
bedside.

So Evald stayed there what time he could,
but never now did Niall stir that evening, but
slept a great deal, and seemed deeper in his
sleep.

"Go," Meara said to him. "Tomorrow the
wedding, Dryw has said. And it would please
him to know. She is a fair child, is she not?"

"Fair to us," Evald said, numb in his deeper
feelings, but Meredydd had settled into his
thinking as she had settled into the hold, without question, because it had to be. "Yes, fair."
His eyes were for Niall's face. And then he
turned away, and passed the door where Scaga
stood watch, haggard and grim and never
leaving.

"He sleeps," he said to Scaga.

"So," said Scaga. Nothing more.

It was a premonition on Evald that he should
not go up to bed tonight, but stay near. He
went down into the wardroom where there was
a fire, and lingered there a time, into the dark
of the night and the sinking of the fire. There

was little murmur from the courtyard or the barracks where Dryw's folk had settled: there was little sound from anywhere.

But the beat of hooves came gently through the dark, gently past the wall, so that it might have been a dream if his eyes had not been open. The hair prickled at his nape and for a moment there was a heaviness over him too deep to throw off.

After that came a scratching at the stones of the wall, and that was too much. He got up and flung his cloak about him, moving quietly, not to disturb the peace. He went out onto the wall, padding softly as he could, unsure whether his ears had tricked him.

Suddenly a darkness bounded up onto the wall, a hairy thing, all arms and eyes. He cried out, a strangled cry, and it leapt back again.

"Cearbhallain," it piped. "I have come for Cearbhallain."

Evald lunged at him: it was too quick and bounded away, but he threw his knife at it. It wailed and dived over the wall, and now everywhere men were crying after lights.

But Scaga reached him first, pelting down the stairs.

"It was a hairy man," Evald cried, "some dark thing—come for *him*; it said, it had come for him. I flung my knife at it—it went down again."

"No," said Scaga. No more than that. Scaga went running for the stairs; but that *no* was one of anguish—of fear, as if he knew the nature of the thing. Evald hurried after, but "Stay by your father," Scaga shouted at him and was gone.

He stood still upon the stairs. He heard the lesser gate open, heard the hoofbeats going away and rushed to the wall to look. It was a piebald horse with something on its back; and after it Scaga ran, down by the river, under the trees.

"Dryw!" Evald shoulted into the yard. "Dryw!"

So it stopped, small and forlorn. The horse had fled, going whatever way it could. And Scaga stopped, crouched near, panting.

"Iron," it wept, "o the bitter iron. I bleed."

"Come back," said Scaga. "Was it for him you came? O take him back."

A shake of the hairy head, of all the body, indistinct in the moonlight, among the leaves. "The Gruagach pities him. Pities you. O too late, too late. His luck is driven all away now. O the bitter iron."

Scaga looked down at himself, his weapons. He laid aside his sword. "That was his son. He did not understand, never knew you. O Gruagach—"

"He is gone," the Gruagach said, "gone, gone, gone."

"Never say so!" Scaga cried. "A curse on you for saying it!"

"Scaga goes wrapped in iron. O Scaga, ill for

you the forest, ill for you. The Gruagach goes back again where you might go, but never will you. Ill for you the meeting. You were never like your lord. Eald will kill you in the day you meet. O Scaga, Scaga, Scaga, they wept for you when you left. And the Gruagach weeps, but he cannot stay."

There was nothing there—neither shadow nor moving branch or leaf, only the moonlight on the river.

And Scaga ran, ran with all that was in him, to reach Caer Wiell.

"He is dead," Evald told him when he came inside, when he had reached the doors. And Scaga bowed down in the hall and wept.

There was a decent time of burying and mourning, and Dryw stayed, buttressing Caer Wiell against its enemies. Evald—lord Evald— with Scaga at his side, dispensed justice, ordered this and that in the lands round about, set guards and posts and took oaths from men that came.

Even from aged Taithleach came a message that only Dryw understood. "The King," said Dryw privily, his skull's-face even more grim than its wont: "this passing has set back the time that might have been. Had your father lived and been strong—but he is gone. Alliances must be proved again."

"Send back," Evald said, "and say that I am

THE GRUAGACH

Cearbhallain's son and the lady Meara's, no other."

"So," said Dryw, "I have done."

And another time: "You cannot go back to your lands," Evald said, "without the promise kept my father made. And I shall be glad of your daughter." It had come to be the truth, for Meredydd had nested in the heart of Caer Wiell to his mother's comfort and to his own, and if it was not love at least it was deepest need. If he had had to sue for Meredydd on his knees now he would have done so; and it was his father's will, the which he tried to do in everything.

"It is nigh time," said Dryw.

So Caer Wiell put off its mourning in the spring. The stones remained, and the grass grew and flowers bloomed, violets and rue.

And vines twined in the wood, among forgotten bones.

BOOK TWO

The Sidhe

NINE

Midsummer and Meetings

Summer lay over the old forest, when leaves veiled the twisted trunks and graced the skeletal branches with a gray-green life. They were stubborn, the old trees, and clung tenaciously to their long existence on the ridge above the dale. There was anger here, and long memory. The trees whispered and leaned together like conspirators in their old age while the rains came and the quick mortal suns shone, and shadows slithered round their roots within the brambles and the thickets. No creatures from the New Forest ventured here without fear; and none stayed the night—not the furtive hare, which nibbled the flowers that stopped at the forest edge, not the deer, which drew the air into quivering black nostrils and bounded away to take her chances with human hunters. Not

the wariest or the boldest of such creatures
which grew up under the mortal sun might
love the Ealdwood ... but there were hares
and deer which did wander here, shadowy wan-
derers with dark fey eyes, swift to run, and not
for hunting.

At rare times the forest seemed other than
sullen and dreambound, and stirred and wakened
somewhat, while the moon shone less white
and terrible. Midsummer was such a time, when
the phantom deer gathered by night, and birds
flew which would never be seen by day, and for
a brief hour the Ealdwood forgot its anger and
dreamed of itself.

On this night, after many such nights, Arafel
came, a motion of the heart, a desire which
was enough to span seeming and being, to slip
from the passage of her time and her sun and
moon which shone with a cooler, greener light,
and out of the memory of trees and woods as
they might have been, or were, or had once
been. She brought a bit of that otherwhere
with her, a bright gleaming where she walked.
Flowers bloomed this magic night which without her presence might never have waked from
their buds, as most flowers did not, in the
Ealdwood men saw. She looked about her, and
touched the moongreen stone at her throat,
which was much of her heart, and shivered a
bit in the cool dankness of a world she had
much forgot. The deer and the hares which,

THE SIDHE

like her, wandered the shadow-ways twixt there and *here*, moved the more boldly for her presence.

Once there had been dancing on such a night, merry revels, but the harpers and the pipers were stilled, gone far across the gray cold sea. The stone at her throat echoed only the remembrance of songs. She came this night out of curiosity, now that she remembered to come. Mortal years fled swiftly past and how many of them might have passed since her grief and her anger had faded, she did not know. She was dismayed. It pained her heart to see this heart of the wood so changed, so choked with brambles. A great mound rose in this place, thorn-ringed now, about which her folk had once danced on green grass, among great and beautiful trees. This night she walked the old dancing-ring, laid a hand on an oak impossibly old, and strength drained from her, greening his old heart and making thin buds swell at his branch-tips. Such magics she had left, native as breathing.

But overhead the stars should have shone clear. Clouds drifted, wrack in heaven. She looked up, wished them gone, that this night be what it ought. The deer and the hares looked up with their huge dreaming eyes, as for a little time the sky was pure. But quickly a wisp of cloud formed again, and fingers of wind drew the taint back across the sky.

"It is long," Death whispered.

She turned, startled, laid her hand on the

stone at her throat, for near the ring had appeared a blot of shadow, a darkness which hovered next a tree the lightning had slain, and for a moment ugly whisperings attended it.

"Long absent," said Lord Death.

"Go from here," she bade him. "It is not *your* night, and not your place."

Death stirred. Deer, beside her, trembled, their shifting steps carrying them nearer and nearer her, and the air breathed with the dankness of most nights in this wood.

"Many years," Lord Death said, "you have not come at all. *I* have walked here. Should I not? I have hunted here. Do I not have leave?"

"I care not what you do," she said. But such was her loneliness that even this converse drew her. She regarded the shadow more calmly, watched it spread and settle on the riven stump as brush swayed. Something doglike settled too, a puddle of shadow at its master's feet. It dipped its inky head and yawned, panting softly in the dark, while the deer and hares froze. "Do not settle to stay, Lord Death. I have told you."

"Proud. Lady of cobwebs and tatters. The old oak is younger tonight. Do you not care to tend the others? Or can it be ... that a little of you fades, each time you do?"

"He is rooted elsewhere, the old tree, and he is more than he seems. Do not set your hand to him. There are some things not healthy for you as well, Lord Death."

THE SIDHE

"For many years, many summers, you have neglected this place. And now your eyes turn this way. Have you cause to come?"

"Need I cause . . . in *my* wood?"

"The Ealdwood is smaller this year."

"It is always smaller," she said, and looked more closely at the shadow, in which for the first time she could see the least distinction, a suspicion of an arm, a hand, but never, never a face.

"Old friend," he said, "come walk with me."

She smiled, mocking him, and the smile faded, for the hand reached out to her. "Upstart youth," she said, "what have I to do with you?"

"You have given me souls to hunt, Arafel. And they are *with* me when I have taken them, but there is no sense in them. No gratitude. And less pleasure. Why do I come? What do you see in your side of Eald? What is there, that I can never see?" The shadow drew itself up, and the hound rose too. The likeness of the hand was still extended. "Walk with me," Lord Death asked softly. "Is it not a night for fellowship? I beg you—walk with me."

The deer fled away, bounding this way and that; the hares darted for cover in panic. The hound stayed, a breathing in the shadow. Suddenly there seemed others of them, a shadowy pack, and the shuffle and stamp of hooves sounded where the darkness was deepest.

A wind started through the trees. Where stars had shone, the blight in heaven had become a dark edge of cloud. Arafel glanced from sky to trees, where the shadows flowed, where small chitterings disturbed the peace.

"Send them away," she said, and the other shadows slunk away, and the wind fell. There was only the greater Darkness, and a chill sense of presence.

She walked with him, from out the ring and more and more solidly within this world where Men lived—incongruous companionship, elven-kind and one of Men's less-reputed gods. He said little. This was his wont, and hers. She had no deep fear of him, for elven-kind had never been subject to him; when their wounds took them, they simply *faded*, and where they went, Death was not, nor ever had been. All had faded now, but she had not; they had gone away beyond the sea, but she had not been willing. She was last, loving the woods too well to go when the despair came on others. It was perhaps habit kept her now; or pride—her kind had ever been proud; or perhaps her heart was bound here. Death had never known the motives of the elves.

She did not walk the shadow-ways, that path which was mostly under her moon. Death could not reach to that other place, and she meant that he never should. She stayed companionable with him, her Huntsman, guardian of her forest what time she was absent, who had come to the land when Men came, and who haunted this forest most of all places on the earth. He

THE SIDHE

showed her the land he had had in care, the great old trees with roots well sunk in her own Eald, that could not easily die. She saw their other selves, their aspect beneath this moon, and now and again she found one dangerously fading, and gave her strength to heal.

"You undo my work," he reproached her.

"Only where you trespass," she said, and looked again at the darkness, wherein two soft gleams seemed to shine. "If I do not go where the others have gone, at the last I shall have drawn all Eald-that-was to heal this blight that Men make; and where shall I be then, Lord Death, having used my strength up so? Is that what you wait for? Do you think my kind can die?"

"I wait to see," he said, and his voice was soft and still. A shadow-sleeve rippled in wide gesture. "All of this you might restore, drive out Men, claim it all, and rule—"

"And die, as it did."

"And die," Lord Death said softer still.

She smiled, perceiving wistfulness. "Merest youth."

"Invite me with you," Death wished her. "Let me once see what you see. Let me see you as you are. Show me . . . that other land."

"No," she said, shuddering, and felt the brush of a touch upon her cheek.

"Do not," Death pleaded. "Do not hate me. Do not fear me. All do . . . but you."

"Banish hope. My kind *fades* from wounds."

"But there is none can wound you," he said.
"None, Arafel. So you are bound here, to share
the fate of Eald."

"There are many who can wound me," she
said, looking placidly toward that place where
she judged a face might be. "But not you."

"Save when the woods are gone. Save when
all that gives you strength has gone. And you
live long, my lady of the fading trees, but not
forever."

"Yet I shall cheat you all the same."

"Perhaps you will." The whisper wavered,
trembled. "Do you know where your kindred
has gone? Do you *know* that that place is good?
No. But me you know. I am familiar and easy.
We are old companions, you and I."

"Companions without fellowship."

"Do you not know loneliness? That, we share."

"But you are all darkness," she said. "And
cold."

"Do all see you the same?"

"No," she confessed.

"Perhaps," he said, "you will come to see me
as I am."

She said nothing to that, for she was not as
cruel as some of her kind, having felt pain.

"I also," he said, "heal."

Still she said nothing.

"Come," he said. "I shall show you my other
face."

She stopped at his touch, for the way to
another, third Ealdwood lay in his power and

THE SIDHE

the wind from it was chill, that place of *his* making. "No," she said. "Not there, my lord, never there."

"What I take," he said, "most oft I return. What comes into the cauldron comes out again. I have a fairer face, Arafel, which you do not know how to see, having no experience of me. You judge me amiss."

"You have done me service," she said, "in defending Eald from Men. Why?"

And now Death was still, giving her no answer.

"Perhaps," she said, "I shall misjudge my time. Perhaps I shall delay in this woods too long. Only that must you hope for. I give you no hope of my consent."

"I have no hope," said Lord Death. Wind tugged at her, drew her farther. "But come, if not to the one place, to the other. I am anxious that you think well of me. See ... that I can heal."

His voice was gentle, promising no ill, and in truth there was none that he could do her. Because she had committed herself the once, she yielded, and walked where he would, as mortals walked, their common ground.

And then she wavered, because she knew where he would lead.

"Trust," he begged of her, and the wind tugged more strongly, insistent and cold.

They walked slowly through the brambles and the thickets, mortal-wise and sometimes painfully; and at the last edge of night they came to that grove he sought, a part of the New Forest, that verge of Eald grown up on the edge of the old, nearest Men. Great trees had died, scarred with axes that she had not forgot. The wanton destruction oppressed her heart, for an edge of her own Eald had died that day these trees had perished, truly died, into that gray haze which bordered all her world and bound her sight.

"See," said Lord Death, and the shadow rippled toward a bank of bracken, lush ferns beneath the dimming stars. Man-tall saplings were springing up through it, straight and new. "See my handiwork. Can we be enemies?"

She saw, and shivered, remembering the place as it had been, when the fallen trees had stood tall and beautiful; and their counterparts in her own Eald had bloomed with stars and sheltered her with their white branches. "It is only more New Forest," she said, "and mine is the smaller for it. They have no roots in Eald."

"You do not see beauty here?"

"There is beauty," she admitted, walking farther, and knelt with a pang of memory, for there were bones and shattered wood beneath the bracken, and she touched a long-broken skull. "The trees, you restored. Canst mend this, Lord Death?"

"In time, even that," he said, twisting yet again at her heart. "Do you care for them?"

The Sidhe

"I have my own cares," she said; but when she had risen, an old curiosity tugged at her heart, and she walked farther with him, to the flat rock which overlooked the dale, upon a dark sea of trees. She recalled the stone keep the other side of the dale—oh, far too well, among villages and fields and tame beasts and all such business as Men cared for. It was all beyond their sight. Below them the Caerbourne rolled its dark flood seaward, a black snake dividing the wood; and that flow toward the sea made her think of endings, and partings from her kindred, and made her sad.

"Men fare as always," said Death. "Borning and birthing and dying. There is no ending of it."

"Yet they end."

"Not forever. That is the nature of them. You will not look on my new woods; it does not please you."

"Not while mine dies."

"Dies and does not fade?"

She looked at him with cold in her heart. "Go away," she wished him. "I am weary of your company."

"You wound me."

"You, spoiler of all you touch? You are beyond wounding. Begone from me."

"You are wrong," said Lord Death. "Wrong about my wounding. There is loneliness, Arafel; and heartlessness; I am never heartless. Beware of pride, Arafel."

"Go hence," she said. "I weary of you."

There was a snuffling in the shadows at her back, a breathing, a chuckling. She frowned and laid her hand on the jewel that she wore at her throat. The sounds diminished. "You do not frighten me, godling. You never did and never shall. Begone!"

The shadow fled, not without a touch, a chill which achieved wistfulness. She waved it away, and knew him truly fled. There was only the hillside, and the spoiled night, and the wind.

She walked along the ridge, having come this far. All the dale was dark before her, mortals still asleep in this their night and her day. She remembered what of hurt and of fairness Men had brought her ... how many of their years ago she did not know. She lingered a time, and a curious longing possessed her, to know what passed there, what manner of thing their lives had become.

TEN

Branwyn

She walked that other way, that slipped with speed no mortal limbs could pace, along paths where brambles did not trouble her. She paused, in the gray glimmering of dawn down the dale, in the pleasant green of new growth, a riverside where she had not come ... in very, very long. She was beyond the present limits of Eald, and yet not, for Eald was where she willed it, and followed her, stretched thin, so that there was effort in this going.

Morning brought mortal beauty, soft touch of sun in golden haze above the black waters of the Caerbourne, beauty of contrasts which her world did not possess, for there was no ugliness there, no dead branch, no fallen tree or unshapely limb. She glanced aside as a shadowy deer followed her out of otherwhere, black

nose atwitch and large eyes full of daybreak.
"Go back," she bade it, for it did not know its
way hereabouts, and it vanished with a breaking of brush and a flesh of dappled rump, which
flickered into the shadow world and safety.

She walked farther, across the water, where
now she could see the grim walls of Caer Wiell
on its hill, with fields spread beyond it like
skirts of gold and green. Evil had lived here
once, surrounding itself with harsh men and
edged weapons. The keep had a new tower,
greater defenses. But today the gates stood
open. New Forest had urged its saplings close
upon this side of the hill, with grass beyond,
and flowers twined upon the grim black stones.
She saw Men coming and going on a path, but
these Men had no hardness about them. They
laughed, and her heart was eased, her interest
pricked as it had not been in long years of Men
. . . for Death's taunting had cast gloom over
her and this sight of life and liveliness was
heart-healing.

A few women sat on the green grass, between the forest edge of saplings and the flower-
twined walls, and a golden-haired child ran
with baby steps on the hillside, laughing. A
strange feeling tugged at Arafel's elvish heart
to hear it, like the echo of such childish laughter in the long ago. She walked out, into mortal sunlight, saw that the child at least saw
her, if others did not. The child's eyes were
cornflower blue and round with wonder.

THE SIDHE

Arafel knelt then and touched a flower, drew a glamour over it, a tiny magic, a gift. The child plucked it and the glamour died, leaving only a primrose clutched in a fat human fist, and dismay in the blue eyes.

Arafel spread the glamour across the whole hillside of primroses, shedding elven beauty on them, and the childish eyes danced for joy.

"Come," whispered Arafel, holding out her hand. The child walked with her into the forest shade, forgetful of flowers.

"Branwyn," a woman called. "Branwyn, don't stray too far."

The child stopped, turned eyes that way. Arafel dropped her hand and the child toddled away, ran at last to the outstretched arms of the woman who had risen to look fearfully into the morning haze amid the bracken.

Human fear. It was chill as Death himself, and Arafel had no love of it. She cast a last longing look at the child and walked away into the shadow of the woods.

"Beware of them," said a whisper at her shoulder. "They die."

It was Death, in the wreckage of an old tree.

"Begone," she said to him.

"They will give you pain."

"Begone, upstart."

"They have no gratitude for gifts," he said.

"The third time—begone."

He went, for at her third command he must, and left a chill behind him.

She frowned and drew back, departing her own way into elven night, and the light of her own and pale green moon.

She thought often about the meeting, but she took her time in venturing again in the face of Death's taunting. Her pride, pricklish elvish pride, refused to acknowledge that he had disturbed her, but she put it off past one midsummer's eve, and yet another, and perhaps more ... time meant little to her, who measured the oldest trees against her lifetime. But at last she came back to that forest below Caer Wiell, dismayed anew to realize how fast human life fled, for the babe was much taller when she had found her again playing on that strip beneath the walls. The child stared at her from wide, little-girl eyes, her doll forgotten in her lap. She had her attendants, who sat to themselves and laughed shrill sly laughs and never saw their visitor. They chattered among themselves, a ring of bright skirts and fingers busy with embroideries. But the child was grave and curious.

And Arafel sat down crosslegged on the ground, let a child show her daisy-chains and how to count wishes. They laughed together, but then the watching girls came and fetched the child away from the forest edge and scolded her.

It was not every day, nor even every moon, that Arafel came. Sometimes other concerns kept her; but she remembered Men more often than her wont in those days, and sang much, and was happy.

Still the mortal time was long; and when at last she delayed for months, the child took her pony into the woods and set out seeking her, along the Caerbourne's willow-shaded banks.

The wood grew darker very soon; and it was no good place to be. The fat pony knew that, and shook her off and raced away in terror. And Branwyn wiped the wet leaves from off her hands and tried to keep her lip from trembling, for what had frightened the pony chuckled and whispered in the bushes nearby.

Many the human intruder in Ealdwood that dusk, with calling and blowing of horns; and they found the poor pony with his neck broken. Lord Evald rode farthest and most desperately, driven by a father's love . . . and Scaga led the searchers farther than most would have dared but for shame to Evald's face and dread of Scaga's anger.

Arafel came looking too, having heard the cries and the intrusion. She found the child tucked like a frightened fawn in the hollow of an old and trustworthy tree, dried her tears, banished the dark from that glade. "Did you come hunting me?" Arafel asked, her heart-touched that at last, after so many years, there was some hope of Men. "Come," she asked of Branwyn, trying to draw her to that place where childhood might be long, and life longer still. But the child feared those other sights.

And suddenly a father's voice rang out, distant through the wood; and the child chose once for all, and called out, and fled for him.

Arafel drew away; and stayed away very long. It was shame perhaps, for intended theft. And pain ... that, perhaps, most of all. Midsummers passed, and beltains, while mortal Eald grew rank and Death did as he would there, failing her presence.

But come she did when her heart was healed. She expected the child where she would always be, at the forest's edge; and when she did not find her there ... at least, she thought, Branwyn would be playing on the hillside on so bright a midsummer day; and finally, seeking with persistence, she went even to the stones of Caer Wiell, man-hewn with painful iron.

So she found Branwyn at last, on the tower's crest, in that sheltered nook where the wind could not reach.

The child's shape had changed. It was a budding woman in a woman's gown, who stared at her in alarm and did not truly remember her, forgetting childish dreams. Branwyn had brought bread there for the birds, and stopped in the very motion of her hand, the cornflower eyes greatly amazed, not seeing *how* her visitor had come, but only that she was there,

THE SIDHE

which was the way most mortals looked at
Arafel when they saw her at all.

"Do you remember me?" Arafel asked, sad-
dened at the change she saw.

"No," said Branwyn, wrinkling her nose and
tilting her head back to stare at her visitor,
from soles of her feet to crown of her head.
"You are poor."

"So some see me."

"Did you beg of me on the road? You should
not have come inside."

"No," said Arafel patiently. "Perhaps you once
saw me differently."

"At our gate?"

"Never. I gave you a flower."

The blue eyes blinked, and did not remember.

"I offered you magic. I did you daisy chains,
and found you in the woods."

"You never did," Branwyn breathed, cupping
the crumbs in both her hands. "*I stopped believing in you.*"

"So easily?" asked Arafel.

"My pony *died.*"

It was hate. It wounded. Arafel stood and
stared.

"My father and Scaga brought me home. And
I never went back."

"You might . . . if you would."

"I am a woman now."

"You still remember my name."

"Thistle." Branwyn drew back, out of her

shadow. "But little-girl playmates go away when girls are grown."

"So I must," said Arafel.

And she began to. But she stopped on a last forlorn hope and cast a glamour as once she had done, on the birds which hovered round about, silvering their wings. Branwyn quickly cast crumbs, and the birds alit and fought for them, so that the gleaming faded in a knot of wings and thieving. She threw more. Such were Branwyn's magics, to tame wild things, by their desires. The cornflower eyes lifted, dark and ill-wishing, conscious of their own power and disdaining forever what was wild.

"Good-bye," said Arafel, and yielded up the effort which held her so far out of Eald.

She faded back then, out of heart to linger there.

"Did I not warn you?" Death made bold to ask her, when next their paths crossed. Then in anger Arafel banished him from her presence, but not from the wood, for she was out of sorts with Men. The dream she had dreamed of humankind had proved more than vain, it was turned altogether against her, like the child who had grown as the saplings had grown in Death's new forest, taking root in this world, and not in hers.

She slipped within the safer, kindlier light of her moon, and into the forest of Eald as her eyes saw it, a forest which had never faded

THE SIDHE

since the beginning of the world, save those areas gone for good. Here all the leaves were silvered in the moon's greener, younger glow; here waters sang, and the birds were free, and the deer wandered with all the stars of night in their eyes.

It was her consolation then, to dream, to walk the woods she loved, and to keep that which remained as it had always been, forgetting Men. Of midsummer nights, sometimes she came, and saw mortal Eald grown wilder and more deserted still. How Death fared, she had no knowledge, nor cared, though it seemed that he fared well, and hunted souls.

ELEVEN

Dun na h-Eoin

The banners fluttered over the tumbled
stones, the watchfires flickered in the dusk,
like stars across the plain. There was war. It
had raged from the Caerbourne to the Brown
Hills to Aescford and south again, for the King
had risen, Laochailan son of Ruaidhrigh, to
claim the hall of his fathers, ruined as it was.

Evald had come, of course. He was among
the first, riding out of Caerdale to forestall the
King's worst enemies in the days before the
King declared himself. He came with Beorc
Scaga's son, and armed men and no few stout
farmers' sons out of the dale, with all the
strength that he could muster. And Dryw the
son of the Dryw of Niall's day, rode from the
southern mountains with the largest rising of
that folk since Aescford. So Luel rose; and Ban;

THE SIDHE

they were expected. Latest came the folk of
Caer Donn, high in the hills: lord Ciaran led
them. Ranged against them were Damh and
An Beag, the wild men of the Boglach Tiamhaidh, and the bandit lords of the Bradhaeth
and Lioslinn.

And the war was long, long and bitter, and
Evald felt little of glory in it: they named him
in songs, but more and more he understood the
Cearbhallain, for what they sang as brave he
remembered most as mud and fear and being
cold and hungry. But all the same he fought,
and when he had time to think at all, he spent
it missing Meredydd and his daughter and his
fireside. He had pains in his joints and his
scars when it rained. A great deal of the war
seemed to be marching and riding, moving
bands of men here and there and forestalling
the enemy at one point to have them break out
in another burning and looting of what they
had lately made safe, so that they had had
great pains to make a border and to hold it, for
the marshes could never be trusted and the
hills were full of warfare.

But at Dun na h-Eoin all that had changed,
where campfires gathered and the enemy massed
so many they looked like a blight upon the
land, their backs against the hills.

Then was a battle, fierce and long, fought
from the breaking of one day to the evening of
the next, and the dark birds gathered thick as

the smoke had been before. But the King prevailed.

"Your leave," Dryw ap Dryw asked of the King that day on the field: "They'll have no rest of me."

"Go," said the King. Dryw was himself pale and spattered with blood, straining at the recall like some hound called back from the hunt. "Keep them on the move."

So Dryw leapt onto his horse and gathered his men about him, afoot, many of them, accustomed to move like shadows among the hills.

"By your leave," said Evald, "I would go with Dryw. An Beag and Damh are old enemies of my hold—and they have force left. The most of my men are here with me; if they should come at Caer Wiell now—"

"We will come at their backs," said the King. "At all possible speed. Let Dryw harry them as he can."

"But Caer Wiell—" said Evald. His heart was leaden in him looking around at the desolation, the clouds of birds flying with the smokes of fires to darken the sky. It was not well to dispute with Laochailan King; he was a man of middling height, Laochailan, fair with eyes of a pale cold blue that never took fire. He had outlived his counselors. They had held him on the leash most of his life, and he was cold, seldom roused. Even in battle his killing was cold; in policy he was deliberate and immovable.

THE SIDHE

And Evald turned his shoulder and strode away with a turmoil in his thoughts. It was treason in his mind, but the will of the Cearbhallain still held him, so that it was would and would not with Evald. He was on the verge of gathering his folk and riding away despite the King; Beorc Scaga's son hurried to his side seeing stormclouds in his eyes, seeing wrack and ruin in the offing, on the bloody field.

"Cousin," the King called after him.

Evald strode to a stop and turned, lifted his head, keeping his anger behind his eyes. "My lord King."

"I will not be scattering my men, some here, some there. You will not be leaving this place without my will."

"Caer Wiell was refuge for your cousin and stronghold for men that held against all your enemies. It holds now against An Beag and Caer Damh and makes their homecoming dangerous. My steward is a capable man to hold against the force they left behind, but he has too few men in his command. I have stripped my land, giving you every man, every weapon I could bring. Now the onslaught comes at Caer Wiell, and what profit to you if Caer Wiell should fall? You would lose all the valley of the Caerbourne; and it would be strong against you—as strong as it ever was for you, lord King, and as dearly bought."

Not even this brought passion to the King's

face. "Do you think to ride against my command, cousin?"

For a moment breath and sense failed Evald. The field, the King, the counselors about him swam in a bloody haze. They were close by the ruins of Dun na h-Eoin: the black birds settled on its broken walls to rest, some too sated to take wing. They began to pitch tents, some bright with the green and gold and most leathern brown, even among the slain, amid the wailing of the wounded. Men removed the bodies, looting them too; or carried the wounded to what care they could give them; or despatched the hopeless or the fallen enemy. That was the manner of the King's war, and the sound and the stink of it muddled the mind and made right and wrong unclear. Evald's hand was on his sheathed sword; and blood had gotten into his glove and dried about his fingers, whether his own or others' he had not yet explored. He thought only of his home, and his eyes saw nothing clearly.

"Will you obey," the King asked, "or no?"

"The King knows I am loyal."

"Then come. Come take counsel with me. Now."

Evald considered, looked at Beorc, Scaga's younger image, beside him. Beorc would ride; and gladly. And thereafter they would be rebels against the King, and no less to be hunted. If they were rebels, then the King might fall, for Dryw would go with them, and so the south-

THE SIDHE

ern mountains and dale would do the thing
that would ally them with An Beag and Caer
Damh, in deed though never in heart. And
perhaps the King saw that looming before him,
since he had called him cousin twice in the
same address and spoke to him courteously.
Laochailan was cold, but he was clever too,
outside the cold determination which had peo-
pled this field with dead. And he knew what
was necessary.

"Come," Evald said to Beorc quietly, and so
they went, across the littered field with its
canebrake of spears standing in corpses, of
tattered banners of the Boglach and the Bradheath, of death and agony.

They had pitched a tent for the King among
the ruined stones of Dun na h-Eoin, in the
courtyard, by the struggling oak which had
somehow survived the fires. They had driven
the pegs between the shattered paving stones
and into what had been a garden. Doves had
sung there. Now carrion crows flapped their
dark and sluggish wings, startled by their
coming. And to this state the King retreated,
drawing with him others of the lords.

As they gathered, Evald glowered about him
and tried to think what there was to do—for he
would far rather now have been the least of
men in Dryw's company than the lord he was.
There was Beorc by him and no other, for he
had no kinsman but the King himself, a king

who would as lief not remember that dark history or how he had come to be. Ciaran of Donn was there with his sons Donnchadh and Ciaran Cuilean, a fey and strange lot. Fearghal of Ban came with his cousins, small dark men and bloody-handed, like Dalach of Caer Luel and his brothers. They were northerners all of them and some from the plains, and none of them had any close ties to the dale or the south.

So perforce Evald came into the tent with them, and bided his time while the King's servants helped Laochailan with his armor and one brought them wine to drink. It was the color of blood. Evald took the cup and it had the taste of it as well, a coppery ugliness in the smoky air, the reek of sweat that was on them.

"Dryw has sped after them," the King said to those who had not been there earliest. "He will keep them moving and never give them rest."

"I say again," Evald began, but Laochailan King turned that pale cold glance on him.

"You have said much," said Laochailan. "You try our patience."

"I serve my King from a hold that has been his from my father's time."

"From the Caerbhallain's," the King said softly, as if it had to be explained, and the color leapt to Evald's face.

"And your cousin's, lord." Evald kept his voice steady, set down the cup and stripped the glove from his hand. Some sword or axe had cut

through the leather. The blood was his. "As
you kindly remember. I ask your leave—no, I
beg it, to go now and keep Caerdale in your
hands. They will join with their own forces.
Dryw may not be enough for them when they
have gained what strength they have in their
own holds. They will gather forces again—"

"Do you lesson me in warfare?"

They were of an age, he and his King, born
near the same year. "I know my lord King has
wide concerns. So I would take this small one
on myself."

"And shall we all go riding to our own holds?"
asked Fearghal. "Two years it has taken to
bring us and the traitors to this field, and lord
Evald would have us go each to his own defense again."

"This field is half empty," Evald said. "The
enemy has gone, has it passed your notice, lord
of Ban? We sit here licking our wounds while
theirs will be healed when they have rein-
forced themselves, and their strength be doubled if they should take Caer Wiell. More than
doubled. In its full strength, Caer Wiell could
hold for longer than we may have strength in
us to hurl against it, with all the Bradheath at
our backs."

"I will not have dissent," said the King. "That
is deadlier than swords. Nor will I release any
but Dryw. His men are light-armed and apt to
this kind of war. You fear too much, cousin.
Your steward is a skilled man in war; and

Caer Wiell has defenders. If anything An Beag
is apt to draw off its attackers to come in our
faces, not against your lands."

"That was not the way I learned An Beag.
No. Pardon me, lord King, but they know the
value of Caer Wiell in their hands, and I know
An Beag, that they will take what chance they
have. Dryw may try but they may hold him in
the hills—and I fear some all out attack against
Caer Wiell before this is done, sparing nothing.
We have hurt the enemy, never killed them. A
wounded beast is still to fear."

"Is fear your counsel then? No, hear me. I
will not divide my forces. I will brook no talk
of it."

"*Set us through the pass*, lord King; and when
you come at their backs then we will be at
their faces. If we are divided, then reunite we
will, over their corpses. But let Caer Wiell fall
and we will leave our corpses at every step we
take into the dale."

The King's fair face never turned color but
his eyes were cold. He lifted a hand that bore
the Old King's ring and silenced the others
with a gesture. "You are too forward. I will not
yield in this."

"Lord," Evald muttered, and bowed his head
and took up his cup again, moved off from the
King's presence, toward Beorc who kept to the
shadow, for he did not trust his wits or his
tongue just now. "Go," he whispered to Beorc,

THE SIDHE

"take horse and take at least the message of what happened here."

"I will," said Beorc, and bowed and was almost out the door with a turn upon his heel, a hasty man like his father.

"*Recall your man*," the King said. "Hold him!"

Spears came down athwart the doorway. "Beorc!" Evald cried at once, knowing Beorc's mind. Beorc stopped but scantly short of harm, and lowered the hand he had almost to his sword.

"Where in such haste?" asked the King. "Dare I guess?"

A lie tempted Evald. He rejected it and looked Laochailan in the eye. "My messengers have the habit to come and go. Should the enemy know more of what was done on this field than my own folk?"

It was perilous. The King's eye had that chillness that went with his deepest wrath. "Cousin," said Laochailan, "messages are mine to send. Do you not agree?"

"Then I beg you send Beorc and quickly. He knows the way."

"I will not have it said a man of this host went home, not the lord of Caer Wiell, not his steward's son, not the least man of his following."

"Lord King," said Ciaran of Caer Donn. "But a messenger—there is treachery in An Beag and Damh. There would be no whispering in the camp at this man's going. It would be well understood—at least by Donn. The dale is at our doorstep, and if Caer Wiell should fall it would be like the old days, with burning and looting in the hills. A messenger to give them heart and ourselves to come at the backs of our enemies—but we will be slow. We have the longer way to go. And what if their heart failed them in Caer Wiell?"

"You make yourself a part of this contention," the King said wryly, and he frowned, for Donn had favor with him. "But Caer Wiell will have no lack of heart. After all, they defend their own lives. And that is trustworthy in these dalemen."

"Lord," Evald said, hot with passion, "but the choice of a defender might be a sortie if he hoped for no help—they are brave, my folk, but they may also be desperate."

"Lord King." It was a voice hitherto unheard in council, Ciaran Cuilean, the younger son of Donn. "You gave your word no man of us should go home before the war is done. But Caer Wiell is not my home. And I know the hills."

There was a deep frown on his father's face and on his brother Donnchadh's. But the King turned to him with his anger sinking. "So. Here is one man who has the gift of courtesy. And one I would be loath to lose."

"Never lost," the younger Ciaran said. He laughed, tallest of all his kindred, fairer than most and more lighthearted. "I have scoured those hills often enough. I can ride through them with less trouble now, if the King will, and maybe quicker than Beorc, who knows? He has not had the hills for his hunting, and I have."

"Then you will carry lord Evald's message," the King said. "Do you frame it for him, cousin, and let us be done with it. I have given you all I will."

A fell suspicion came on Evald then—that his cousin the King had some fear of him, feared messages and secrets passed—feared this kinship with him. It was a dark thought and unworthy. Others followed it, as dark and fearful. He drove them all away. "Lord King, my lord of Donn, my gratitude." He worked the ring from his finger. "My steward's likeness you can know from his son. Show this to him. Speak to my lady: I send this ring to her. Tell her how things stand. That whatever they hear they must hold a little time, and the King will be coming at An Beag from the back."

"Lord," said the younger Ciaran, taking the ring, "I will."

"There will be peril in it," Evald said.

"Aye," said Ciaran, just that, which so quietly spoken mended all his thoughts of Donn.

"Speed well," Evald said earnestly, "and safely."

"Your leave, sir—lord King." So Ciaran embraced his father, but his brother would not, and excused himself to the door of the tent.

"I am in your debt," said Evald quietly. His pride was hurt, and anger still rankled in him,

for it was less than he had wanted. A terrible
fear was in him that the King wished the war
to go toward the dale and batter down its
strength awhile, for it was too rich and too
well-situated and its lord was a kinsman. But
that was too dire, even thinking what the war
had come to. It was too great a waste. He
looked on the young man Ciaran as young and
high-hearted as once he had been, and all his
heart went with the man as he walked from
out the tent and into the dying day. But he
ached with his wounds, and there was counsel
to be held. He set his hand on Beorc's shoulder,
silently wishing him to peace, and Beorc's arm
was hard and stiff with anger.

So the King took counsel of them, how they
should map the last assault on An Beag and
Damh and the Bradhaeth, while the cries of
the wounded and of the carrion crows mingled
in the evening. Evald shivered and drank his
wine. He served the King as his father would,
if he had lived to see the day; and for his
mother's sake; and little for his own.

"That is a good man they sent," Beorc said
quietly while the King called for wine. "They
speak well of the youngest son of Donn."

"So shall I," Evald said, "of all Donn, ever
after this."

As for Ciaran, he delayed little in his going,
seeking after the best horse he could lay hand
to, taking his brother's shield with the cres-

THE SIDHE

cent moon of Donn upon it, for his own was broken.

"Take care," his brother said, Donnchadh, dark as he was fair, less tall, less favored by the King or even by their father.

"I shall," Ciaran said soberly, seeing to the gear, and took the wineflask his brother pressed on him. "That will come welcome on the trail."

"You should have kept silent. You never should have thrust yourself into this."

"It is no small message," Ciaran said, "the saving of the dale."

"He never trusts the dale. Never. It is unsavory. And never you forget it."

"I shall not," Ciaran said, and hung the shield on his saddle, with the parcel of bread and meat a servant brought him. He slung his sword there too, and turned and embraced his brother longer than his wont at partings. "Evald galls the King. But that is not saying he is no true man, far too true to lose. . . . Keep you safe, Donnchadh."

"And you," his brother said, holding him by the arms. "You take it far too lightly. As you take everything."

"And you are far too worried. Is this more than riding into the same hills with the enemy in strength in them? More to fear is Dryw: I should hate him to take me for some wild man of the Bradhaeth. Keep yourself safe. I will see you at Caer Wiell—and I shall have been din-ing on plates and sleeping in a fine soft bed, while you shiver in the dew, Donnchadh."

"Do not speak of sleeping."

"Ah, you are too full of omens. I shall fare better than you do, and worry more for you before the walls than myself behind them. Only see that you come quickly and we will push the rascals north and be done with them. Be more cheerful, Donnchadh."

So he took his leave, and flung himself into the saddle and rode away, taking the longer path at first, which was less littered by the dead and seeming-dead. The smokes of fires lit the hills, campfires and the fires lit by the pit where they dragged the dead.

It was not an auspicious hour. He would gladly have rested. But he served the King and lived to do it when others he knew had not. And he had to take Dryw's way through the hills and not fall into ambush, either of Dryw or An Beag.

He lost no time in going now, through the wrack of war. Truth, he was not as light about the matter as he had told Donnchadh, but he saw ruin in delaying the army at Dun na h-Eoin, ruin for more than Caer Wiell. It was twice Laochailan's failing, to delay too long upon a field and throw away half of what they had gained; and the dale was too close to Donn. Now it was rushing all downhill, the King on the verge of moving. He was, he hoped, the first pebble before the landslide—for now Donn

THE SIDHE

would give the King no peace. And so they
would remember this ride of his, he thought,
for he rode to herald not alone the battle for
the dale, but what might well prove the telling
battle of all the years of war.

TWELVE

The Faring of
Ciaran Cuilean

It was not so swift a ride, from Dun na
h-Eoin's ruins through the hills. Once Ciaran
met with Dryw's folk, but only once, and that
was to his liking, for the southrons were sudden men and apt to haste in their killings. He
suspected their presence sometimes, a silence
of birds where birds ought to sing, a strangeness in the air that he could not put name to.
But at last he had passed all of that manner of
thing and reckoned that he was past Dryw's
farthest easterly advance—for Dryw would go
off to the north direct to the Caerbourne as the
enemy had fled, while his own course cut deeper
into the woods.

But at last he reached the river himself, and
forded it, choosing rather the hazards of the
far shore than the ill repute of the southern

one. He had been in the saddle so long he had forgotten when he had rested—his resting when he took it was only for the horse, and then he was back in the saddle again, sleeping little, aching with the weight of the mail and of his bruises from the battle. Now he kept the shield uncased on his arm, trusting none of this dark wooded way through the vale of the Caerbourne. He was in the dale now. There were no friends hereabouts. He watched about him, no longer hoping that Dryw was close. This was the darkest, the most dangerous portion of his ride. He had managed it so that he reckoned to pass An Beag in the dark, and hoped that he knew well enough where he was.

The day waned, and at times the horse faltered on the narrow trail, which ran over stone and through woods, along the black waters of the Caerbourne, which rushed and splashed over rock in its shallow places, frothing white in the gathering murk. The brush was too thick here for his liking though it offered him cover. He was a horseman; he preferred something less tangled than this thicket, which wore at the horse and in places made every step a risk, in which their moving sounded all too loud. Least of all did he like the whispering that filled the twilight here, rustlings not of the horse's making, little movings which seemed wind alone, and might be something else. All this forest was a place of ill legend; and they

did not love such legends in his hills, in Caer
Donn, where the old powers were still dreaded,
where ruined towers and strange stones poked
from out the gorse and broom and reminded
them of all things older than the gods, old as
stone and like the stone, everywhere underfoot.
There were places in his own hills he would
not ride by twilight, not for any cause; and
names not for speaking by dark or brightest
day. The terror was as close here. The horse,
long-ridden and drenched in sweat as it was,
still threw its head and rolled its eyes and
stared into this shadow and the other, nostrils
wide. Where it could it kept a steady pace
through the forest shadow, a panting rhythm
of leather and metal and the beat of hooves.

Then two pale moths came flying, a whip-
ping arrowsound ... Ciaran flung up the shield;
and a blow jarred it, while the horse reared up
and leaned leftward in a sudden loosening of
life.

He sprawled clear of the dying horse, shield
lifting, jarred by a second shaft thumping into
the wood while others hissed through brush
and his back hit the thicket. He scrambled
desperately to cover himself and to run, tore
his ungloved right hand on thorns, while the
crash of brush warned him of enemies coming.
His back met a tree and he braced himself
there on his feet. He had his sword from sheath,
and they came on him in a mass in the forest
dark, with staves and knives. Blows battered

at his shield, and he hewed at them with every stroke that his weary left arm could gain him room to take—the blade bit and there were screams. They tried to come at him from behind, and he swung with his shoulders still to the tree and killed one of them and another, rammed his shield under a bearded chin and hewed again, with ebbing strength, for there was a quick numbing pain in his side and he knew something had gotten through, in the joinings. An axe swung down on him, shivered the top of the shield and stuck fast. He let the shield go and swung the sword two-handed, clove ribs and wrenched the blade free in backswing, while a staff came down on him. The blow dazed him; but he rammed the blade's point into that one's belly and slew him too . . . while brush crashed and cries were raised beyond—*Help, ho! help, we have him!*

He took to the brush and began to run, staggered across the thigh-deep rush of the Caerbourne, chilled and sodden, waded ashore and set out running on the other bank, sought brush again when arrows hissed after. Voices cursed in the gathering dark. He sought higher ground with a wildling's instinct, not to be driven into some hole against the stream's winding banks. Branches tore at him and snapped. His limbs turned leaden with the weight of armor, and his side ached. A veil seemed fallen over his eyes and the little light in heaven was dimmed, all murky, yet for a time he ran with hope, for it seemed that his pursuers had fallen behind. He climbed, took ways closer and closer with brush and twisted, aged trees, through tangles so dense that even bracken would not grow, past stony upthrusts and over jagged ground. He hoped; and then the brush about him crackled to a dry chuckling, and the wind stirred through the branches like a rising storm. He ran farther, until all the sound in his ears was his heartbeat, and the brush breaking and his own harsh breath tearing his throat.

But another breathing grew at his heels, the whuff of a running horse, the beat of hooves which broke no brush as it came.

He spun about to face attack, but there was nothing there but the blackness, and the wind and a cold which settled about his heart. Then he feared as he had never feared in battle, and ran as if effort before this were nothing. The ache in his side was more than want of breath; he pressed his swordhand's wrist there and felt the ebb of blood.

He was weakening. He heard a chuckling and now knew the name of that rider which followed him, and the name of the wood into which he had strayed. And when he was nigh to falling he set his back against an aged tree in a space clearer than the others, where it seemed that he might at least have the grace of seeing his enemy come on him.

Shadow came, and a spatter of rain, a rattle of thunder, and the baying of hounds. Shadows flooded among the trees, black bits of night which rushed and leaped for him. His sword swept through them, nothing hindering, and a coldness fastened and worried at his arm, numbing all the way to his heart.

He cried aloud and tore free, ran, leaving a fragment of himself in the jaws, and the sword was no longer in his hand. The shadows coursed behind him, and the hoofbeats rang like the pulse in his ears and the hoarse breathing was like his own. The enemy was not behind him, but lodged in his side, where the wound worked at his life. A part of his soul was theirs, and they would tear him to nothing when they came on him again, a rending far worse than the first. Rain spattered into his face and blinded him, dampened the leaves so that they clung to him and his armor was soaked so that he did not know now what was blood and what was rain. He stumbled yet again, in a crash of thunder, and of a sudden as surely as there was a horror behind him he conceived of safety in the trees ahead, where seemed a mound overgrown, a swelling of the land with life, where the trees grew vast, and strong, stretching out their limbs in sympathy.

He reached it, entered it, sped in strange freedom of limb where trees were gnarled and straight at once, barren and flowered with stars, and aglitter with jewels like hanging fruit, with treasure of silver laid upon the white branches, swords and shining mail, cloth like morning haze, spiderweb among pale green leaves.

A sword hung before him, offered to his hand ... he tore it from the leaves in a scatter of bright foliage, and the brightness about him faded, leaving him alone with the dark and the swift loping shadows, with the dark rider, who burst upon him in a flickering of lightnings and yet absorbed no light himself, like a hole in the world through which he might fall forever, if the hounds did not have him first. He held the illusory blade trembling before him, and shuddered as its light drew detail from the dark, of jaws and eyes of hounds. He was drawn to look up, to lift his face unwilling, to face the rider—he saw something, which his dazed mind would not recall even in the instant of beholding it.

The rider came closer, and a chill came on his flesh, on all but the hand which held the blade. He lost the brightness, could not hold even his vision of this grim place. The black began to come over him, but he slashed at it and the hounds yelped aside from him, bristling and trembling.

"Come," a voice whispered to him, very softly.

He must, for he could not hold his arm up any longer. The blade wavered, and sank, and yet a warmth broke like a breath of spring at his back. "Stand firm," someone said.

"He is mine," said the shadow, a voice like shards of winter ice.

"Be off," said the other, soft and without doubt.

"He has stolen from you. Do you encourage such thefts?" And for a moment the world was bright, and the shadow was a blight upon it, a robed darkness which stood in an attitude of amazement. "Ah," the cold voice breathed, wonder-struck. "Ah. *This* you have kept from me."

Light blazed. Ciaran staggered in it, and his knees hit the ground, a shock which wrung a sob of pain from him, and he could no longer tell earth from sky or day from night. Wet leaves lay against his cheek or cheek against the leaves, and the rain beat down into his face, chilling his torn soul.

But the shadow was gone, and the thunder stilled. It seemed the moon shone down. A face confused itself with it, and with the sun in a strange, fair sky.

He still clutched the sword. Slim cool fingers pried his hand from it, eased his limbs, covered him with a downy peace in which the only pain was to his heart, an ache and a memory of loss.

THIRTEEN

The Tree of Stones and Swords

She knelt with the rain still dripping off the leaves, a dew upon them both, and very still and pale the intruder lay beneath the mortal moon. Iron tainted him, and yet he had torn through into her forest—if only for a moment; had brought iron there, and Death. She was stirred to anger, and to fear, and to a longing which had not been in her heart since the child had broken it. To have entered her Eald, to have found that very heart of it and to have stolen an elvish sword ... it was no common thief, this Man, and no common need could have forced him. Perhaps his mortal eyes had been affected by that terrible wound he bore, so that he fled with truer sight than most; but never in many a hunt had Lord Death failed.

Eald had stretched far once, before the coming of Men; and once, before her folk knew much of Men, there had been a few of halfling kind, for elvish loves and dalliances among these fatal strangers. Still, she thought, there might be elvish blood drawn very thin in some, halflings who had never felt the call across the dividing sea, who had never faded. In hope she tried to draw this stranger with her, but the iron weighted him and he could not stay.

She endured the anguish of handling it, undoing buckles, putting it off him, every bit and piece. So she uncovered a terrible wound in his side, and drew on her power to begin its mending, healed the little scratches with a single touch. And when she had rested a moment, it was not hard to bear him away with her, simply a holding of his head in her lap, and a thinking on elvish things. Then the trees became what they truly were, straight and beautiful, and the sun of her day shone down with kindly warmth in that grove.

He slept long, while the wound healed itself, while the lines of mortality faded from his face and left it beautiful, with that beauty which might be elven heritage. She did not leave him in all this time, waiting for his waking with all her heart.

And at last he did stir, and looked about him, and looked into her eyes, seeming much confused. He began at once to fade into the mortal world, into darkness, being in his own mind again, but she took his hand and drew him back before he could slip away. "Beware of going back," she said. "Death has a part of you. Too, too easy for him to call you into his shadow as you are. You are much safer here."

He tried to rise, still holding to her hand, maintaining that delicate hold on *here*. She lent him strength, the green force which sustained the trees themselves, and after a moment he was able to stand and to look about him. Wind whispered through the leaves and the sun cast its own glamour, while deer stared at them both wise-eyed from the green shadow, in the grove of swords and jewels.

"I was dead," he said.

"Never," she assured him.

"My heart hurts."

"So it may," she said, "for it was torn. And that healing is beyond me.— What is your name, Man?"

Dread touched his eyes. "Ciaran," he said then quietly, as a guest ought. "Ciaran's second son of Caer Donn."

"Caer Donn. Caer Righ, we called it, the King's domain."

He feared, but he looked her in the face. "And what is your name?" he asked.

"I shall tell you my true one, that I do not give to mortals; for you are my guest. It is Arafel."

"Then I must thank you with all my heart,"

THE SIDHE

he said earnestly, "and then beg you set me on the road from here."

In so many words he healed her heart and wounded it . . . and a regret came into his eyes as if he had seen the wounding. He held up before her his right hand, on which he bore a golden ring, worked with a seal.

"I have a duty," he said. "On my honor, I have to go and do it, if there is still time."

"Where is this duty?"

He lifted a hand as if he would give a direction, and nothing was the same. "There are armies," he said in his confusion, pointing where he might mean the Brown Hills. "There is war on the plain; and my King has *won*. But the enemy has drawn off this way, which is a valley where they might hold long in a siege if they could take it. And lord Evald of Caer Wiell is riding with the King. Do you understand, lady Arafel? War is coming up the dale. Caer Wiell must not be deceived. They must hold firm, whatever the false reports and fair offers from the enemy, must hold only a little time, until the King's army comes this way. Lord Evald's hold—must hear the message I bear."

"Wars," she said faintly. "They will not be wise, who set foot in Ealdwood."

"And I must go, lady Arafel. I must. I beg you." Already he began to fade, discovering the power of will within himself.

"Ciaran," she said, a summoning, and held him by his name, still within the light of her sun. "You are determined. But you do not count the cost. The Huntsman will seek you out again. Once in the mortal world, you are a prey to him; he has never lost a hunt, do you see? And it is not finished."

"That may be," he said, pale-faced. "But I have sworn."

"Pride," she said. "It is empty pride. What arms have you, what means to pass through all of Eald against such enemies?"

He looked down at himself, armorless and empty-handed. But he wavered toward a parting, all the same.

"Wait," she said, and went to the old oak, took from its branches one of the jewels which hung among the others, pale green like the one which hung at her own throat, though dimmed, for its master was ages gone. It sang to her, the dreams of an elf named Liosliath, a part of his soul, such souls as her kind had. "Take it. You borrowed his sword in your need, but this will serve you better. Wear it always about your neck."

"What are these things?" he asked without taking, and looked about at all the trees which held such treasures, jewels and swords glimmering silver and light among the leaves. "What place is this?"

"You might liken it to a tomb; this you robbed

... my brothers and my sisters, my fathers and mothers. It is elvish memory."

"Forgive me," he whispered, stricken.

"We do not die. We go ... away; and when we are gone, what use are these things to us? Yet they hold memories. That is their use now. The sword, you could not fully use. But take this stone. Liosliath would not grudge it to a friend of mine. He was my cousin: he was young as our kind go, and so it may be safest for you. The shadows feared him."

He took it in his hand, and his eyes widened and his lips parted. Fear ... perhaps he felt fear. But he held it fast, and it sang to him, of elvish dreams and memories.

"It too is power," she said. "And danger. It does not make you a match for Death; but 'twill fight the chill ... if you have the heart to use it."

He gathered the silver chain and hung it about his neck. His fair clear eyes clouded in the power of the dreams. But he was not lost in them. She touched her own dreamstone, and called forth the faintest of songs, a sweet, bright harping. "Do not trust in iron," she warned him. "That and this ... do not love one another. And come, since you must. Come, I shall walk with you on your way. Eald will take you there more safely than you might walk in the world of Men."

"This is given for a baneful place," he said.

"Walk it with me, and see."

She offered her hand. He took it, and his was warm and strong in hers, human-broad but comfortable. He walked with her, and for all his apprehension a wonder came into his eyes when he saw the land, the trees of elven summer, the glamoured meadows abloom with glistening flowers, the timid, wide-eyed deer which stared at them as they passed.

Stone sang to stone, his heart to hers, and the wind grew warm beneath that other sun. She felt something which had long frozen about her heart melt away, and she knew companionship for the first time in human ages, a fellowship lost since Liosliath himself had faded, last of all elves save herself.

("Forgive me," Liosliath had said, this Man's unwitting words and her cousin's last, which had tugged at her heart. "I have tried to stay." But he had had that look in his gray eyes which was the calling, and once it had begun in his heart, the fading began, and all her wishing could not hold him—nor could she go with him, for her heart was here.)

"It is beautiful," Ciaran said.

"Not so wide as once," she said. And, remembering: "We held Caer Donn once."

"The grandfathers say—there are your sort still there."

She tossed her head, stung. "Faery folk. Silly nixes. And sad. They have few wits. They

The Sidhe

shapeshift so often they forget themselves and cannot get back again—That is not to say they are not dangerous when crossed."

"That is not your kind."

"No," she said, laughing, in better humor. "Not mine. We were the greater folk. Elves. The Daoine Sidhe. The faery-folk live in our ruin. They never loved us."

"And others of your kind?"

"Gone," she said. "But myself."

He let go her hand to look at her, and in letting go he drifted, cried out in fear, for they were on Caerbourne's edge, a bright stream, willow-bordered, and here its name was Airgiod, the Silver. She took his hand again and steadied him.

"Beware such lapses. You might fall. Caerbourne has eroded deep in human years, and his banks are steep. And worse, far worse, there is no knowing how deep he has sunk in the shadows. Lord Death's geography is a darker mirror of this, but mirror nonetheless, and I should not care for *his* river. Remember your wound when you walk in Eald."

He shivered; she felt the dread keenly, a chill in the stone upon her breast. She touched it and warmed it, and him.

"Use the stone," she bade him. "He shall not have the rest of you if you know how to walk in Eald. Your heart's wish can bring you here, only so you do not stray too far; your heart's wish can take you away."

"It is a great gift," he admitted at last. "But they say all gifts in this world have cost."

"Not among kinsmen."

He looked up at her as deer look at hounds, wary and distraught.

"There's elvish blood in you," she said. "Do you not know? You could not have come, else. We once ruled, I say, in Caer Donn."

"So they say." She felt the beating of his heart, like something trapped in the stone within her hand.

"Is it so terrible," she asked, "to discover such a kinship?"

"I am my father's own son, no changeling."

"Then by father or mother, you carry blood of mine. You are no changeling, no. There is nothing of the little folk about you. Is it sire or mother stands taller than most?"

Fear filled him, a tumbling down of all truths he knew. *Father*, she thought, catching this from his mind. He said nothing. She felt a chill in him, self-aimed. She perceived memories of old stones near Caer Donn, recollections of child-hood terrors, of ill legends and human hate, and shivered herself.

"I am sorry," he said, sharing this. His mind was awash with fear, and with thoughts of his own duty, and of dying, and the black hounds. He touched the chain of the stone about his neck, making to draw it off, but she caught his hand and gently forbade that.

"You will not die," she promised him. "I will take you where you will go. Come, it is not far."

The forest edge lay up the bright stream-course, that place where sight stopped in mist, the edge of her world. She led him into that gray place, walking blind, but one hand she kept on the stone which remembered the world as it had been, and so she brought some substance out of nothingness, enough to find her way beyond the edge. She remembered Caer Wiell as it had once been, a fair green hill with a spring never failing; and so she came to it, and still held his hand fast. Half in the shadow-ways there was a dimming, a glare of fire, the shouts of war, ghosts of battle swirling about them.

Other things were there too. Death was one. "Pay him no mind," she said to Ciaran, who turned and faced the shadow. "No. Hold to the stone and come with me."

She set them more and more surely in mortal night, with the din of war about them, with Caer Wiell's black walls above. She knew the gateway. It did not have wards against her. She set him through.

"Fare well," she said. "And fare back again."

So she stepped clear of Caer Wiell, back into the swirling shadow-din outside.

She felt a presence by her, a shadow which had drawn a moment out of the battle, a blackness sullen and cold.

"Hunt elsewhere," she told him.

"You have had your will," Lord Death said, making ironic homage.

"Hunt elsewhere."

"You give this mortal uncommon gifts."

"What if I do? Are they not mine to give?"

The shadow said nothing, and she walked away through the grayness, and into bright Eald, into her own. The phantom deer stared at her curiosly in elven sunset; and she walked back to the grove of the circle, touched the stones which hung from the ancient oak, harked to precious memories which they sang as the wind blew among them. One voice was stilled now from the chorus, that which had been Liosliath's.

"Forgive," she whispered to him, who was far across the dividing sea, far from hearing her. "Forgive that it was you."

But a strange companionship shivered through her still, after ages in solitude. She walked, and mingled with the eldritch harping which was the peculiar song of her stone of dreams, came the whisper of another heart, human-tainted, but true as earth. She was appalled somewhat at the nature of it, for he had known war; he had killed—but so had she, in the cruel, cold anger of elves. Human anger was different, all blood and blind rage, like wolves. He knew passions she felt strange; he knew strange fears; and self-doubts. It was all there,

THE SIDHE

drowning Liosliath's clear voice. He feared
Liosliath; he denied, human-stubborn, the
things his own eyes had seen in Eald.

But there was no hate in him.

She sank down at the base of the tree of
memory, and drew her cloak about her, and
dreamed his dream.

FOURTEEN

Caer Wiell

They brought him as a prisoner into the torchlit hall, with the sounds of battle dying. They had handled him ungently, but it was their lord's own ring upon his finger, and they had changed their manner quickly enough when he insisted to show them that. "Sit," they told him now, showing him a bench, and he was only too glad to do so, weary as he was.

Another came—Old wolf, Ciaran thought at that grim broad face, besweated and flushed with battle-heat. He straightened himself at once when that man came in with more men-at-arms behind him. He set himself most carefully on his feet. "Scaga?" he ventured, for he was very like his son, a huge man and red-haired. "I come from the King; and from your lord."

THE SIDHE

"Let me see his ring," Scaga said; and Ciaran thrust out his hand, which the old warrior took roughly, turning the ring to the firelight. Scaga let it go again, his scarred face still scowling.

"I have a message," Ciaran said, "for your lady's ears." And because he could guess the keep's want of hope: "Good news," he urged on Scaga, though he was charged to take it higher.

"Then it comes welcome, if true." Scaga turned his face toward the open door, where sounds of battle had much faded, then looked back again, looked him up and down. "How came you here?"

"My message," he said, "is for lord Evald's lady."

Scaga still frowned; it might be the nature of his face, or of his heart: this was, Ciaran thought, a fell man to cross. But Evald trusted him as steward, in a hold beset with enemies: he was then a man of great worth and faithfulness.

"With neither armor," said Scaga, "nor weapon. . . . How came you into the courtyard?"

"Your lord's ring," Ciaran insisted. "I speak only to your lady." He felt the stone which lay hidden within his collar, a presence, a warmth which seemed greater than natural. It frightened him, with that against his heart and the like of Scaga staring into his eyes, full of suspicions.

"You shall go to her," Scaga said, and motioned to the stairs. "Boy!" he called. "See my lady roused."

A lad scampered up the steps at a run. Ciaran shivered in weariness and cold, for wind blew through the door. He wished desperately for a cup of ale, for a place to lie down and rest himself.

And there was none, for Scaga looked on him with narrowed eyes and offered nothing of hospitality—motioned men-at-arms to go before and behind him and led him up the steps to another hall within Caer Wiell's thick walls, which at least was warmer, with a fire blazing in the hearth.

"Beware," a voice seemed to whisper in his hearing, and it startled him. He wondered could all the rest hear it; but the others did not turn: it was for him alone. "Beware this hall. They do not love elven-kind. And do not show them the stone."

A stone wolf's-head was set above the fireplace. It seemed he had seen it before; that he had sat here, a man, and that a harp should hang so, upon the rightward wall—he looked, and was dismayed to find a harp hanging there, just where he had thought it should. He had then dreamed this place.

Or she had. There was a great scarred table where once had sat a chair, before the fire. He blinked it clear, went to it, leaned there wearily against the table, while weary men guarded him.

And women came, so soon that he supposed they had not been asleep. Surely they had not been, with the enemy hurling fire against the hold. They came from the inner door which opened on this hall, one woman older and somewhat grayed. This was Meredydd, he surmised, Evald's own lady; and *Meredydd* the stone whispered in his heart, confirming it. The other of the twain was young, bright of hair—and that name came whispering through his heart as well: *Branwyn*. Branwyn. Branwyn. He stared without meaning to, for so much of anguish and of anger came whispering with that name. This Branwyn stopped and stared at him, blue eyes seemed bewildered and innocent of such pain.

"Your message," Scaga's harsh voice insisted.

Ciaran looked at Lady Meredydd instead, took a step toward her, but hands moved to weapons about him, and he did not go nearer. He tugged the ring from off his finger and gave it over to Scaga, who gave it to the lady. She took the ring as something precious, looked on it closely, lifted anxious eyes. "My husband," she asked of him.

"Well, lady, he is well. I bring his love and my King's word: Hold, defend, and do not be deceived by any lies of the enemy or accept any terms. The King has won a great battle at Dun na h-Eoin, and the enemy hopes for this valley as their last holding place. Only hold this tower, and the King and your lord will come as soon as possible against their backs. They know this. Now you do."

"Now bless your news," the lady wept, and even Scaga's frown was eased. Meredydd came and offered her hands to him in welcome, but he felt Scaga's heavy hand on his shoulder, pulling him away.

"There is more to hear," said Scaga. "This man came over the walls somehow, with no armor, no arms—unmarked through the lines outside. There are questions should still be asked, my lady, however good and fair the counsel seems. I beg you, ask him how he came."

For a moment doubt shadowed the lady's eyes.

"My name is Ciaran," he said, "Lord Ciaran of Caer Donn is my father. And as to how I came—lightly, as you see; by stealth. While your enemies struck at the gates—I came another way. I shall show you. But armed men could not take it."

He was not used to lies. He felt fouled, wounded when the lady pressed his hands. "You will show us where," Scaga said, and gave him in his turn a bearish embrace, gazed at him with emotion welling up—hope, it might be, where hope had been scant for them before. Branwyn too came and kissed his cheek; and weapons were done away as men came at last to clap him on the back and to hug one another for joy. A cheer lifted in the hall, and there was such desperate happiness—He felt a stirring through the jewel too, a presence, a distressing realization that he had said nothing

THE SIDHE

on his own which ought to have convinced them
and so relieved their hearts, but that some
strangeness overlay him and his words, makng
them better than they were.

They gave him wine, and brought him upstairs to a princely room—her lord's when he
was young, the Lady Meredydd said; and true,
everything there showed some woman's love,
the fine-pricked stitchery of coverlet and tapes-
tries, the hangings of the bed. Branwyn herself
brought a warm rug for the floor, and maids
brought water for washing, while Lady Meredydd
with her own hands brought him bread hot
from the morning's baking. He took it gratefully,
while the lady and her daughter lingered to
ply him with questions, how fared Evald and
kinsmen, cousins, friends, men of the hold, a
hundred questions during which maids eaves-
dropped and men-at-arms contrived to listen
on pretext of errands. Some few men he knew;
sometimes the news was sad and pained him;
and most often he knew only a name, or less—
but it gave him joy when he could report some
loved one safe and well. Scaga's son was one,
for Scaga bent enough to ask. "He is well."
Ciaran said. "He led a good portion of Caer
Wiell's men at Dunn na- h-Eoin, first of those
that broke the shields of the Bradhaeth while
lord Evald cut off their retreat. He came out of
the battle well enough; he was by lord Evald
when we parted, in the King's own tent." The

old warrior did not smile to hear it, but his eyes were bright.

"He must sleep," Meredydd declared at last. "Surely he has travelled hard."

"I fare well enough," Ciaran said, for he ached after human company, for noise of voices, for all these sights and sounds of humankind.

"Before he sleeps," said Scaga, "he must show us this weak place in our wall."

The warmth drained from him. He nodded consent, not knowing what he was to do, but compelled to go. He swallowed a bit of bread gone dry in his throat, drank a last sip of the wine and set the cup down. "Aye," he said. "Of course. That will not wait."

Scaga rose, waiting at the door. Ciaran took his leave of the ladies, walked with the old warrior through the hall, his heart beating hard within his breast.

"I do not know if I can find it easily," he said to prepare his excuse, and hating the lie. "From all the turnings of this place inside ... I cannot be sure."

Scaga said nothing, which seemed Scaga's way. It gave him no comfort. And when they had come up on the walls, Ciaran looked about him in deep distress, seeking something to confirm his lie.

"Look east," the softest of whispers came to him, like the touch of a breeze. "Turn east and look down."

He walked that way along the battlement,

THE SIDHE

with Scaga treading heavily beside him. He paused at a place and looked down, where the stonework of the walls was oldest and roughest, where here and there brush had rooted itself in the gaps between the stones and man-made walls thrust crazily above the jagged stone of the underlying rocks. Of a sudden his eye picked out a way, weaving from one such foothold to another among brush rooted in the wall, a peril to the hold. "There," he said. "We are a mountain hold, we of Caer Donn. And I climbed cliffs as a lad. There, do you see, Scaga? There and there and there."

Scaga nodded. "Aye. That does want clearing, and watching. Our eyes must have been blind to it. A man sees things too often and so not at all: I had not marked how the brush had grown."

"Rains, perhaps," Ciaran said hoarsely, but in his heart he knew differently. He shivered, for his wool shirt was not enough against the wind, and felt Scaga's friendly grip fall upon his shoulder.

"Come. Our thanks, young sir. Come in."

He walked, glad of the wind-breaking shelter of walls on the one side of the battlements, gazed back as they walked, and suddenly down at an opening out of the walk. The courtyard was below, jammed with livestock and with village folk, a noise which welled up at him thinly, the wail of children and the listless bleating of goats. But it was a well-ordered place, Caer Wiell, and some of the men on the

walls were country folk, light-armed, but goodly
looking men, quick of eye and brisk about their
business. Women were climbing up the inside
scaffoldings which gave access to the battlements before the gates, bearing baskets of bread.
There was then no hunger here, nor would
there ever be thirst, because of the spring which
named the hill, out of reach of the enemy.
Ciaran felt much cheered by what he saw of
the defense, even with the ominous smoke of
enemy fires rising before the walls. He walked
farther out than Scaga would have had him go,
walked the wall to the area of the main gates
and looked west.

Then he was less cheered, for the extent of
the black ruin before the walls. The grass and
fields were burned and trampled into mire.
The enemy had carried away their dead and
wounded; no corpse was left but the carcasses
of slain horses, to draw the black birds; and
beyond that trodden ground the hills were
seared with fire, villages and farms burned,
surely, from here to Caer Damh. The smoke
rose in countless plumes from the hills, where
a vast host camped, a crescent of smokes from
the Caerbourne's forested verge to the barren
hills to the right, that spread itself on the
winds and darkened the sky.

The attack could not have been this far advanced when he was on the road, riding from
the King. He had passed one night—surely one
night—in Eald.

THE SIDHE

How much of time? he asked that sometime whisper in the stone, feeling uncertainty all about him. *How long did you hold me?* He was betrayed. He knew it in his worst fears.

The fires would soon grow more and more, as Dryw and the King over the hills drove others into retreat. Or had it happened already? And what more had happened, and what men he just had named living might have died? And what stayed the King from coming?

Hold here. How old was the message, that Scaga was so grim, that lady Meredydd and her daughter caught so desperately at this hope he gave them? And how long had the King delayed to come?

"It seemed the fires had grown in number," said Scaga out of his silence. "Now we know why."

"Aye," Ciaran said, wishing to say nothing at all.

He went back into the tower, and sat in the hall at the table by the fire, victim again of questions from those humbler folk who had not asked them before; and a few common folk who served there came only to look at him with their hopes unspoken in their eyes, and to steal quickly away. He sat there most of that long day, alone some of the hours, and sitting with Scaga in the afternoon, who brought some of his trusted men to question him at length—how great the strength of the enemy, what condition their arms, what number yet might come. He answered what questions he could as wisely as he could, hinting nothing, and was glad when they had gone away.

No more of lies, he wished of Arafel. You have tangled me in lies, more and more of them. They break my heart. What is truth? What should I say to them? Should I make them doubt the very hope I came to give them?

She had no answer for him, or did not hear.

But that evening after supper a young man came and took down the harp from the wall, and played songs for him and for the ladies. Then he felt a warmth near his heart, a sweet, sad warmth. Then was peace, for the first time in the day. From the enemy there was no stirring, and the pure notes of the harp found another rapt listener; a joy flooded back from the stone, and filled Ciaran's heart. He smiled.

And looked by chance into Branwyn's eyes, who smiled too, in her hope. The smile faded to gravity. The eyes stayed upon his, flower-fair.

"No," a whisper came to him from the depths of the stone.

The blue eyes were nearer, and had a glamor of their own. He gazed entranced while the harper sang.

"Cling to the stone," the whisper came again, but he had Branwyn's fair hand within closer reach of his upon the table. He touched her fingers and they clung to his. The harper sang of love, and heroes. Ciaran held her hand for

THE SIDHE

more tangled reasons, that it was of this world, and that it too had power to hold.

At length the harper ceased. Ciaran drew back his hand, lest others remark it, for she was a great lord's only daughter, however dire the times.

And in time he went alone to his bed in the room which had been Evald's in his youth, the vast soft bed of broidered hangings. He stripped off his clothing, shivered in the wind which blew in out of the dark, through the slitted window—stripped off all that he wore but the stone on its silver chain and lay down quickly, drawing the heavy quilts over him, tucking up his limbs until he could warm him a spot in the bed. He reached out again to snuff the wick of the lamp on the table, drew the arm quickly back beneath the covers, as dark settled strange shapes over the unfamiliar objects of the borrowed room. There were creakings and movings, from outside and in; a child cried somewhere in the dark, from the courtyard on the other side, far, far away. His own slit of a window faced the river. He heard a distant whisper of leaves or water: wind, he thought; and somewhere hounds belled, a sound greatly out of place in besieged Caer Wiell. He clutched the stone in his hand, drew warmth from it, and no longer heard the dogs.

* * *

He dreamed of groves, vast trees; and of a hill. This was Caer Wiell; but he called its name Caer Glas, and there was no well, but a clear spring bubbling out over white stones, flowing unhindered to Airgiod's pure waters in the vale, and the view was clear and bright toward the Brown Hills. He rode the plain, tall and bearing the same pale stone on his breast— rode among others, with the blowing of horns and flourishing of banners. Arrows came down like silver sleet, and the sullen host before them fled, seeking the mountains, the dark places at the roots of the hills. The Daoine Sidhe warred, and in the sky glittered the jeweled wings of dragons, serpent-shapes passing like storm in the blowing of horns and the clash of arms.

Then were ages of peace, when the pale sun and green moon shone down without change, and harpers sang songs beneath the pale, straight trees.

There came the age of parting, when the world began to change, when Men came, and Men's gods, for the vile things were driven deep within the hills, and Men found the way now easy. Came bronze, and came iron, and some there were of the Sidhe who abided the killing of trees, small wights who burrowed in the earth close to Men; but the Daoine Sidhe hunted these, in bitter anger.

Yet the world had changed. The fading began, and the heart left them. One by one they fell to

THE SIDHE

the affliction, departing beyond the gray edge
of the world. They took no weapons with them;
took not even the stones they had treasured—
for it was the nature of the fading, that they
lost interest in memory, and in dreams, and
hung the stones to stay in rain and moonlight
to console those still bound to the world. Most
parted sadly, some in indirection, simply bewildered; and some in bitter renunciation, for
wounded pride.

He felt anger, a power which might have
made the hills to quake—Liosliath, the stone
whispered in his mind, and he drew breath as
if he had not breathed in a long, long age, and
looked up and outward, forcing shapes to de-
clare themselves in the mist which had taken
the world, trees and stones and the rush of
wind and water.

Ciaran waked, caught at the bed on which
he lay, all sweating and trembling, for his heart
beat in him far too loud. He stared into the
shadowed beams above him, wiped the sweat
from his face with hands callused and coarser
than the hands he had had in his dream, rested
them on a body rough with hair and sweating,
with the pulse jarring at his ribs—not at all
the body he had worn in the dream, slim and
shining fair, with the stone aglow with life and
light, with bright armor and a slim silver sword
which shadows feared and no Sidhe enemy
wished to face.

Liosliath, star-crowned, prince of the Daoine
Sidhe, the tall fair folk.

And himself, who was earthen, and coarse,
and whose power was only that in his arm and
his wits.

He shivered, sweating as he was, and tears
ran from the edges of his eyes. He tried again
to sleep, and dreamed of Arafel, of sunlight
and silver, and the phantom deer leaping in
and out of shadow, for it was her waking and
his night. The pale elven sun shone, blinding,
and she walked the banks of Airgiod, up to the
point where it faded into mist and nothingness,
as near to him as it was easy for her to come.

Kinsman, she hailed him. It was as if she
had suddenly turned her face toward him. He
waked with a start in his own darkness, and in
trembling, put off the stone, laid it and its
chain on the table by the bedside, by the lamp.
He wished no more such dreams, which tor-
mented him with what he was and was not
and could never be, which thrust an elflord into
his heart with all the melancholy doom of the
fair folk, all their chill love and colder pride.
They were dread enemies when stirred: he knew
so; and so, he thought, might *she* be, who had
been kind to him.

Kinsman she had hailed him; but it was
Liosliath who was her cousin, Liosliath whose
cold pride wished to live again, Liosliath, the
terrible bright lord whose sword had slain Men.

"A terrible enemy," a shadow whispered.

Tʜᴇ Sɪᴅʜᴇ

And far away, even waking, Arafel cried to him: "The stone, Ciaran!"

He was dreaming then. He was naked and a part of him blew in tatters. There was a forest like the Ealdwood where a wild thing fled, and he was that creature. Limbs rustled, black branches, and even the leaves were black as old sins; the sky was leaden, with a moon like a baleful dead eye.

"Terrible," it said again, and a wind blew through the inky leaves.

Behind him. It hunted him and he must not look at it, for he was in its land, and if he saw the enemy's true face it would be real.

"The stone!" a voice wailed on the wind.

He reached for it, straining all his heart into that reaching. It met his fingers, and his hand glowed with that moonbright fire. Shadows yielded, as he retreated out of that third and dreadful Eald. He passed other creatures less fortunate, shadows which cried and pleaded for aid he could not give. Elf prince, some wailed, asking mercy; elf prince, some hissed, spitting venom. He dared not shut his eyes, dared not look.

Then he lay again within walls of stone, and Arafel's voice was chiding him. He shivered in his borrowed bed, with the stone safe in his fingers. He lay shivering, with sullen day breaking through the windowslit. A chill breeze stirred his hair. Thunder rumbled outside.

He took the cold silver chain in his hands

and slipped it again about his neck, lay still a time holding to the stone with both hands, shivering at the flood of elvish memories . . . of old quarrels with this shadow-lord. The courage seemed bled out of him, through the wounds the hounds had made in his soul. He knew himself maimed—maimed forever, in a way which others could not see and he could not forget. The stone must be forever about his neck to shield him, and it was more powerful than he. His hands were cold that clutched it, and would not warm easily; they were mortal, and that jewel was elvish memory—of one who had not loved Men.

He stirred at last, hearing others astir in the keep, the calling of voices one to the other, ordinary voices, recalling him to a world no longer fully his. He rose, his teeth chattering, and pulled on his breeches and went to the windowslit, hugging his arms about him. He saw the muddy hill, the forest verge, wet green leaves and gray sky. Of attackers there was no sign but the marks which had been there before. The rain was nothing but dreary mist. He turned back and sought after his shirt and the rest of his clothing. He tucked the stone within his collar, tied the laces which concealed it at his throat. He dared not leave it . . . ever.

FIFTEEN

Of Fire and Iron

The ladies were in the great hall to give him morning's hospitality. Meredydd and Branwyn and their maids; and two of the pages had stayed to serve them. He walked among them with a hope of a seat near the fire and a bit of bread crowded upon him; but there were places laid at the table, and he heard the lady Meredydd send a page for porridge. Scaga appeared in the door as the boy dodged and scurried mouselike about his errand, and nodded a good morning. "All's quiet," Scaga said. There was no great joy in the report, and Ciaran frowned too, wondering how long till it came down on them doubled. Perhaps the enemy had no liking for rain. Perhaps—the thought came worrisome at his empty stomach—there was something else astir. Perhaps something had gone amiss with the King, some trick, some trap prepared. The King, Dryw, his father—should come soon. They should make some move.

Perhaps—the thought would not leave him— they had tried and failed while he slept in Eald, unknowing. Some ambush in the lower end of the dale could have prevented them. The desolation before the walls of Caer Wiell was as wide as that at Dun na h-Eoin—and he could not judge whether the enemy was greater in the dale than they had reckoned in the first place or whether the forces fled from Dun na h-Eoin had joined them.

He sat where the Lady Meredydd bade him, at her right; and Branwyn sat at her left. Scaga sat down too, and others, but many seats at the great table stayed vacant, the hall of a hold long at war, its lord and young men absent. The harper sat with them, late arrival; there was the Lady Bebhinn, elderly and dour; and Muirne, all of twelve, who was a shy, pale-cheeked child, silent among her elders. The hall at Caer Donn came to his mind unbidden, his parents' faces, the laughter of servants, joyous mornings, full of noise, himself and dour Donnchadh always at some friendly odds over trivial things. But it would be lonely there this morning too.

"You did not rest well," the demoiselle Branwyn said, who sat facing him. Her face was troubled.

THE SIDHE

"I slept," he said, straightening his shoulders; but the stone seemed a weight against his heart. And because his answer did not seem to satisfy those who stared at him: "I ran far—in coming here. I think the weariness has settled on me."

"You must rest," said Lady Meredydd. "Scaga, no harrying of him today."

"Let him rest," Scaga replied, a deep rumbling. "Only so *they* do."

The porridge came. Ciaran ate, small familiar motions which gave him excuse not to talk. In truth he felt numb, endured a moment's fear that he might have begun to fade into elsewhere, so distant he was in his thoughts. He imagined their dismay if he should do so.

And in this homelike place he thought a second time of home, and meetings. Of facing his father and mother and Donnchadh, bearing an elvish stone forever against his heart, with close knowledge of that past which Caer Donn tried never to recall. He could never again see the farmer's wards against the fair folk without feeling his own peace threatened; could not see the ruins on the mountain above Caer Donn without seeing them as they had been before any Man set foot there; could not walk the hillsides without knowing there were other hills within his reach, and knowing what fell things swarmed beneath them, never truly gone. Worst, to face his father and Donnchadh, knowing what they must never know, that he and they were closer to those things than ever they had believed, these things which lurked and crept at the roots of the hills; and to look on his father's and his brother's faces and to wonder whether the taint always bred true.

Unsavory, Donnchadh had called the date—but he must live with an enemy always a breath away, Man's shadow enemy, who would take the rest of him—without the stone.

Then he looked about him at the faces of the folk of Caer Wiell, whose war was the same as his, but without such protections as the stone; it was the same Enemy. Death had been outside the walls yesterday, hunting souls. Do we not, he wondered, all bear the wound? And am I coward, because my eyes alone are cursed to see him coming?

The stone seemed to burn him. "Be wise," a whisper reached him. "O be wise. He is *my* old enemy, before he was yours. He wants one of elven-kind. Me he waits for . . . and now you. Your fate is not theirs. Your danger is far more."

He touched the stone, wished the whisper away. I am Man, he thought again and again, for the green vision was in his eyes and the voices about him seemed far away.

"Are you well?" asked Lady Meredydd. "Sir Ciaran, are you well?"

"A wound," he said, bedazed into almost truth, and added: "Healed."

"The rain," Scaga said. "I have something

will warm the aches.—Boy, fetch me the flask from the post downstairs."

" 'Twill pass," Ciaran murmured, ashamed; but the boy had sped, and the ladies talked of herbs and wished to help him. He swallowed sips of Scaga's remedy then, and accepted salves of Meredydd and the maids; and before they were done, warmer clothing and a good cloak all done with Meredydd's own fine stitching. Their kindness touched his heart and plunged him the more deeply into melancholy. He walked the walls alone after that, staring toward the camp of the enemy and wishing that there were something his hands might do. All the mood of the keep was grim, with the drizzling rain and the unaccustomed silence. Women and children came up onto the walls to look out; and some wept to see the fields, while youngest children simply stared with bewildered eyes, and sought warmer places again in the camp below.

Beyond the river he saw the tops of green trees, and shadowy greater trees high upon the ridge beyond the Caerbourne, over which the clouds were darkest. Those clouds cast a pall over his heart, for it was Death's presence, and the castle was indeed under siege by more than human foes. The thought came to him that he might bring danger on others, that Death who hunted him might take others near him. This enemy of his might bring ruin on Caer Wiell, on the very folk he came to aid. The thought began to obsess him and cause him deeper and deeper despair.

"Come back," a voice whispered to him, offering peace, and dreams. "You've done your duty to Caer Wiell. Come back."

"Sir," said a human, clear voice, and he turned and looked on Branwyn, cloaked and hooded against the mist. He was dismayed for the moment, and recovering, made a bow.

"You seemed distressed," she said. "Is there moving out there?"

He shrugged, looked across the wall and turned his gaze back to her, a pale face framed in the broidered mantle, eyes as changing as the clouds, mirroring his own fears, unfearing while he was brave, frightened when the least fear came to him. "They seem to have no love of the rain," he said. "And your father and mine, and the King himself—will come soon and teach them other things they will not be fond of."

"It has been so long," she said.

"It cannot be much longer," he said in desperate hope.

Branwyn looked on him, and on the field before them, and they stood there a time, comforted in each other. Birds alit on the stone . . . wet and draggled; she had brought a crust of bread with her, and broke it and gave it to them, provoking battle, damp wings and stabbing beaks.

"Enchantress," Arafel breathed into his heart.

THE SIDHE

"They have stopped being honest; and it has always amused her."

But Ciaran paid the voice no heed, for his eyes were on Branwyn, discovering how graceful her face, how pale on this gray day, how bright her eyes which surprised him with a direct glance and jarred all his senses.

A boy ran, scurried past them and stopped where they stood; he pointed silently and hastened on. With dread Ciaran turned and looked beyond the walls, for in that moment there was change. A group of riders had come out from the enemy camp, advancing toward the keep. There began to be a stirring in Caer Wiell as other sentries saw it. He looked back at Branwywn, and so distraught was her face that he reached out his hand to comfort her. Her chill fingers closed about his. They stood and watched the enemy ride closer.

"They wish to talk," he said, seeing the fewness of the riders. "It is no attack."

Scaga came thumping up the steps to the crest of the wall, leaned over the battlement and glared sourly at the advance. "My lady," he wished Branwyn, looking about at them both, "I would have you back under cover. I do not trust you to luck. I would not have you seen."

"I shall stay," Branwyn said. "I have my cloak about me."

"Stay away from the edge," Scaga bade her,

and stalked along the wall, giving orders to his
men.

The enemy came into clear view, a score of
riders bearing banners, most of them the red
boar of An Beag, and the black stag of Caer
Damh. But they had another banner trailing
crosswise of a saddlebow, and this they lifted
and showed. A cry of rage went up from the
walls of Caer Wiell, for it was the green banner of their own lord.

"Surrender," one rider of An Beag rode forth
to shout against their walls. "This keep is
yielded; your lord is dead, the King fallen, and
his army scattered. Save your lives, and those of
your lord's wife and daughter—no harm will
come to them. Scaga! Where is Scaga?"

"Here," the old warrior roared, leaning out
over the stones. "Take that lie hence! We name
you the liars you are, in the one and in the
other."

A second rider spurred forward, and lifted a
dark object on a spear, a head with hair matted with blood, a ruined face. He slung it at
the gate.

"There is your lord! We offer you quarter,
Scaga! When we come again, we will not."

The lady Branwyn stood fast, her hand limp
in Ciaran's; but when he gathered her against
him for pity, she failed a little of falling, and
hung against him.

"Ride off!" Scaga roared. "Liars!"

A bow bent, among the riders. "Ware!" Ciaran

cried, but Scaga had seen it, and hurled himself back from the edge as the shaft sped, a flight which hissed past and spent itelf. Arrows sped from the walls in reply, and the party rode away not unscathed, leaving the green banner in the mud, and a bloody head at Caer Weill's gates.

"These are lies!" Ciaran said, turning to shout it over all the range his voice could reach, to walls and the courtyard below. "Your lord sent me to forewarn you all of tricks like these—a false banner and some poor wretch's ruined face—these are *lies!*"

He was desperate in his appeal, only half believing it himself. The whole of the keep seemed frozen, none moving, none seeming sure.

"When was there truth in An Beag?" Scaga roared at them. "Trust rather the King's own messenger than any word from them. They know they have no other hope. The King has won his battle. The King is coming here, with our own lord beside him, with Dryw ap Dryw and the lord of Donn. Who says he will not?"

"It was not my father!" Branwyn shouted out clear, stood on her own feet and flung back her hood. "I saw, and I say it was not!"

A handful cheered, and others followed. It became a tumult, a waving of weapons, a hammering of shields by those who had them.

"Come inside," Ciaran urged Branwyn, and took her arm. "Haste, your mother may have heard."

"Bury it," she said, shuddering and weeping, and Ciaran looked at Scaga.

"I will see to it," Scaga said, and with a word to his men on the wall to keep sharp watch, he went down the steps to the gate. Ciaran wrapped the corner of his cloak about Branwyn and walked with her inside the tower, into torchlight and warmth, and up into the hall, to bear the news themselves.

But he went down again when he had seen Branwyn to her mother and given report, into the court where Scaga stood.

"Was it?" he asked Scaga when he could ask with none overhearing.

"It was not," Scaga said, his eyes dark and grim. "By the way of an old scar my lord has I know it was not; but no other feature did they leave him. We buried it. Our man or theirs—we do not know. Likest theirs, but we take no chances."

Ciaran said nothing, but turned away unamazed, for he had fought the ilk of An Beag for years, and still it sickened him. He yearned for arms, for a weapon in hand, for an answer to make to such men. It was not the hour for it. No attack was coming. Their enemy meant they should brood upon what they had seen.

There was silence all the day. Ciaran sat in the hall and drowsed somewhat, with moments of peace between visions of that gory field and more terrible visions of silvered leaves, of all

THE SIDHE

Eald whispering in anger beyond the walls. He would wake with a start and gaze long at something homely and real, at the gray of a stone wall, or the leaping of flames in the hearth, or listen to the folk who went about their ordinary business nearby. Branwyn came to sit by him, and that peace too he cherished.

"Ciaran," a faint voice whispered from time to time, destroying that tranquility, but he refused to pay it heed.

They placed double guard that night, trusting nothing; but there was firelight and comfort in the hall. Ciaran recovered his appetite which had failed him all the day, and again the harper played them brave songs, to give them courage: but the stone plagued him—in his ears echoed other songs of slower measure, of tenor never human, of allure which made the other songs seem discordant and sour. Tears flowed down his face. The harper misunderstood, and was complimented mightily. Ciaran did not gainsay.

Then must be bed, and loneliness and the dark—worse, the silence, in which there were only inner echoes and no stilling them. He was ashamed to ask for more light, like a child, and yet he wished he had done so when all were abed and he was alone. He did not put out the light, having trimmed the wick to nurse it as long as he he might. The stone and he were at war in the silence, memories which were not his nor even human, memories which grew stronger and stronger in the long hours of solitude, so that even waking was no true defense against the flood of images which poured down upon his mind.

Liosliath. He felt more than memories. He took in the nature of him who had worn these dreams so many ages, a pride which reckoned nothing of things he counted fair—which flung against them elvish beauties to turn them pale, and showed him the sadness in his world. He tried taking off the stone with the light there to comfort him, but that was worse still, for there was that aching loss, that knowledge that a part of him was in that darker Eald. Worst of all, he felt a sudden attention upon himself, so that the night outside seemed more threatening and more real, and the light of the lamp seemed weaker. He quickly placed the chain back about his neck and let the stone rest against his chest, which warmed the ache away ... and brought back the tormenting bright memories.

Then the light guttered out, and he sat in the dark. The room was very still, and the memories grew harder and harder to push away.

"Sleep," Arafel whispered across the distance, with pity in her voice. "Ah, Ciaran, sleep."

"I am a Man," he whispered back, holding to the stone clenched in his fist. "And if I yield to this I shall not be."

Music came to him, soft singing, which soothed and filled him with an unspeakable weariness, lulling his senses. He slept without

THE SIDHE

willing to, and dreams crept upon him, which
were Liosliath's proud self, burning pride and
sometimes heartlessness. He longed for the sun,
which would make real the familiar, common
things about him; and when the sun came at
last, he bowed his head into his arms and did
sleep a time, true sleep, and not a warfare for
his soul.

Someone cried out. He came awake with
brazen alarm clanging in his ears, with cries
outside that attack was coming. "*Arms!*" echoed
down the corridors of Caer Wiell and up from
the distant court. "*Arm and out!*"

Fright brought him to his feet, and then a
wild relief, that it was come to this, that it was
no more an enemy within him, but one that
yielded to weapons such as human hands could
wield. He tugged on his clothing, raced into
the hall with others, and finding no Scaga—
down the stairs as far as the guard room. Scaga
was arming, and others were.

"Get me weapons," Ciaran begged of them;
and Scaga ordered it. Boys hastened about meas-
uring him with their hands, seeking what armor might fit him. Outside the alarm had
ceased. The battle was preparing. The room
had a busy traffic of boys running with arrows
and the air stank of warming oil. They began
to lace him into haqueton and leather, and one
of the other pages came up panting with an
aged coat of mail. Ciaran bent and they thrust

it over his arms and head; he straightened and it jolted down over his body with a touch like ice and poison. "No," he heard the whisper which had been urging at him, ignored. "*No*," he raged in his own mind, with the poison seeping into his limbs and weakening them. Tears came to his eyes, and a bitter taste to his mouth, the harsh sour tang of iron. They did the laces, and he stood fast; they belted on the sword, and by now Scaga, armed, was staring at him with bewilderment, for his limbs had weakened and sweat poured on his face, cold in the wind from the door. The pain grew, eating into his bones and through his marrow, devouring his sense.

"*No*," he cried aloud to Arafel; and "no," he murmured, and crashed to his knees. He bowed over, nigh to fainting, consumed with the pain. "Take it off, *take it off me.*"

"Tend him," Scaga ordered, and hesitated this way and that, then rushed off about his own business, for by now the sound of the enemy was a roar like many waters, and out of it came nearer shouts, and the angry whine of bows.

The pages loosed the belt and loosed the laces, pulled the iron weight off him while he knelt, racked with pain. They brought him wine and tended him among the wounded which began to be brought in from the walls. "See to *them,*" Ciaran cried, clamping his teeth against the poisoned anguish in his belly. Tears of shame stung his eyes, that they delayed with him, while others died. He gained his feet and held to the stones of the wall, sweating and trembling. He made his way out into the open air to use a bow, that much at least. But when a boy gave him a case of arrows, the iron sickness came on him again: the case spilled from his hand and the arrows scattered on the walk. "He cannot," someone said. "Boy, get him hence, get him up to the hall."

He went, steadied by a page on the stairs, staggering because of the pain in his bones. The boy and the maids together laid him down by the fire, and pillowed his head.

"He is hurt," came Branwyn's voice, all anguish for him, and gentle hands touched him. A halo of bright hair rimmed the face which bent above him, against the fire. Tears blurred his eyes, pain and shame commingled.

"No hurt touched him," said a boy. "I think, lady, he must be ill."

They brought him wine and herbs, covered him and kept him warm, while he hovered half-sensible. Outside he heard the clash of iron, heard battle shouts and heard the reports of boys and maids as they would scurry out and back again, how the battle leaned, this way and that. For a time the tower echoed to a crashing against the gates, and there was a dread splintering which brought him off his pallet and to his feet. The words were in his mouth to beg a weapon of them, but the pain in his bones urged otherwise. He hung there against the wardroom door and listened to reports more and more dire shouted up the stairs, for one of the great hinges of the gate had given way beneath the ram, and they braced it as they could, with timbers, and hailed arrows from the wall.

There were ebbs in the battle. Ciaran sat by the fire and pressed his hand against the stone which lay unseen against his breast, but it was silent, giving back only pain. She is wounded too, he thought, with only slight remorse. He was alone in the hall but for Branwyn and the Lady Meredydd, who stared at him with bewildered eyes when they did not go down to tend men more bloodily wounded.

All that day the battle raged about the gate. Men died. At times Ciaran rose and walked down as far as the edge of the wall, but men-at-arms urged him to go back again to safety, and the sight he saw gave him no comfort. The battered gate still held, though tilted on its hinges. Arrows sleeted both up and down the wall, and there was desperate talk of a sortie, to get the enemy from before the gate before it should fall entire.

"Do not," he wished Scaga in his mind, but he could not pass that arrow storm to reach the place where Scaga stood above the gate. Scaga was wise and ordered defense and not attack; oil rained down and discouraged those below, but then the enemy set fires before the gate and the oil made them burn the more fiercely. Another hinge had yielded by afternoon, and more and more the enemy came. Wounded men, exhausted men, passed Ciaran empty-handed in his vantage place, some looking on him with bruised and accusing eyes. Women came up the scaffolding to carry arrows, stayed to tend wounds, to take bows, some of them, behind wickerwork defense, and sent shafts winging into the thick press of attackers. Ciaran came out at last, took a bow from a wounded archer, tried yet again; one and a second shaft he launched ... but the sickness came on him, and his third went far amiss, fell without force, while the bow dropped from his hand across the crenel. A boy took up the bow, while Ciaran rested there overcome by shame, until he found the strength to carry himself back to shelter.

They brought the boy back later, dead, for a shaft had struck him in the throat, and another, younger boy had taken his post. Ciaran wept, seeing it, and stood in the corner in the shadow, wishing to be seen by no one.

He heard at twilight the battle din diminished; and at long last it faded entirely. He went back to the hall, to stand near the warmth of the fire and hear the servants talk. The women came, weary and shadowed-eyed, and there was talk of a cold supper from which no one had heart. Men were down in the courtyard trying to brace up the gate, and the sound of hammers resounded through the hall.

Scaga came up, pale and sick from an arrow which had pierced his arm and drawn a great deal of blood. From him Ciaran turned his face, and stared into the embers as he leaned against the stones of the fireplace. The ladies sat; servants brought bread and wine and cold meat.

Ciaran came to table and sat down, staring at what was before him and not at the women, nor at the harper, who had fought that day; nor at Scaga, at him least of all. The servants served them, but no one touched the food.

"It is his wound," Branwyn said suddenly, out of the silence. "He is *ill*."

"He claims to have run through enemies and scaled our wall," Scaga said. "He gives us fair advice. But who is he, truly? How far did he run? And what manner of man have we taken among us, when our lives rely on a gate staying shut?"

Ciaran looked up and met Scaga's eyes. "I am of Caer Donn," he said. "We serve the same King."

Scaga stared at him, and no one moved.

"It is his wound," Branwyn said again. He was grateful for it.

"We have seen no wound," said Scaga.

"Would you?" Ciaran asked, for he had no lack of scars. He put on a face of anger, but it was shame that gnawed at him. "We can go

into the guardroom, if you like. We can speak
of it there, if you like."

"Scaga," Branwyn reproved the old warrior,
but Lady Meredydd put a hand upon her
daughter's, silencing her. And Scaga put himself on his feet. Ciaran stood, prepared to go
down with him, but Scaga beckoned a page.

"Sword," Scaga said. The boy brought it from
the doorway. Ciaran stood still, not to be made
a coward in their eyes. Branwyn had risen to
her feet, and Lady Meredydd and the others,
one after the other.

"I would see you hold a sword," Scaga said.
"Mine will do. 'Tis good true iron."

Ciaran said nothing. His heart shrank within
him and the stone already pained him. He
looked into the old warrior's eyes, knowing the
man had seen more than the others had. Scaga
unsheathed the sword and offered it toward his
hands; he reached for it, took the naked blade
in his palms, and tried to keep the anguish
from his face. He could not. He offered it back,
not to dishonor the blade by flinging it, and
Scaga took it gravely. There was a profound
silence in the room.

"We are deceived," Scaga said, his deep voice
slow and sad. "You brought us fair words. But
gifts of your sort do not come without cost."

There was weeping. He saw the source of it,
which was Branwyn, who suddenly tore herself from her mother's arms and rushed from
the hall. That wounded as much as the iron.

"I told you truth," Ciaran said.

There was silence.

"The King," Ciaran said, "will come here. I am not your enemy."

"We have lived too long next the old forest," said the Lady Meredydd. "I charge you tell me truth. Is my lord still alive?"

"I swear to you, lady, I had his ring from his own hand, and he was alive and well."

"By what do the fair folk swear?"

He had no answer.

"What shall we do with him?" Scaga asked. "Lady? Iron would hold him. But it would be cruel."

Meredydd shook her head. "Perhaps he has told the truth. It is all the hope we have, is it not? And we need no more enemies than we have. Let him do as he wills, but guard him."

Ciaran bowed his head, grateful at least for this. He did not look at Scaga, nor at the others, only at the lady Meredydd. Since she had nothing more to say to him, he walked quietly from the hall and upstairs to imprison himself in the room they had given him, where he was spared the accusation of their eyes.

Dark had fallen. There was no lamp burning in the room, nor did he reckon that any servant would come to him tonight. He closed the door behind him, gazed at the window through a haze of tears. The night was bright, framed in stone.

Branwyn wept somewhere, betrayed. The joy

THE SIDHE

he had brought them all was gone. They expected now to die. He shut his eyes, seeing his own family, the pain he was sure to bring them. Shame, and grief more piercing than shame, that they would forever know what they were and distrust their own natures.

He sat down on the bed in the dark, and unlaced his collar, drew forth the stone and held it in his hands.

SIXTEEN

The Paths of Eald

"Arafel," he whispered, "help us." But no answer came, and Ciaran had hoped for none. It was doubt, perhaps, which robbed him. He felt a pain in his heart, pain in all his joints, as if the poison of the iron he had touched had gone inward. Perhaps it had more than driven Arafel away; perhaps it had wounded her more than he had known. There was silence, where once her voice would have come whispering to him, and he was afraid.

The stone was power. She had promised so. To cast it off, seek a death in battle ... he thought of this, foreknowing that he would see before his death what others could not see, and know it when it came. It seemed a small-hearted thing now, though lonely; a selfish thing, to perish to no avail, and to take the hope of Caer

THE SIDHE

Wiell with him once for all. Power was for using in such straits as he had set them in, if he but knew how.

And what had the stone ever done, but link him to Eald? *Fare back*, Arafel had wished him.

He began, holding the stone between his hands. He rose and slipped his mind toward the green fair world ... saw gray brightness, and moved into it.

There was nothing here. He tried to recall the way he had come with Arafel's leading. He thought that it lay before him in the mist. A certain sense of his heart said so, and he trusted that sense, which he had denied before.

Liosliath, he thought, wishing now for the memories of that grim elf, but nothing came to him. It was, perhaps, the taint of iron. Panic swept on him like a flood of water. He wavered out of the mist and blinked in dismay, for he stood on the dark slope of the hill, outside the walls of Caer Wiell.

In panic he reached for the mist again, and ran into it, ran, with all his strength, but very quickly he was lost indeed, and he was not sure that he had taken the right course in the beginning. He thought that he could see trees in the grayness, but they were not straight and fair, but twisted shapes, and the mist darkened.

Shadows were with him, loping along in

dreamlike slowness. He could not see them well, but he heard the crash of brush, the beat of hooves, slow and strange. A stag coursed the mist, but it was black, and lost itself in the grayness. A bird flew past, baleful-eyed, and black as the stag. It called at him and flew on. He ran the more, panting, and at times his feet seemed to lose their purchase and to stride lower than he wished. Hounds bayed, striking terror into his flesh, and his wound grew into an ache, and to agony. He heard the beat of heavier hooves, and the winding of a horn.

Something tattered swept by him, wailing. He stumbled away from it and shuddered against another shadow, saw trees taking tortured shape. The way was darker and darker, agreeing with mortal night, as the elven-wood never had. He was possessed of sudden terror, that he had fled the wrong way altogether, that he was driven and harried where the enemy would be, toward a place where the stone had no power to save him. A wind blew which did not scatter the mist, but chilled him to the bone.

"Arafel!" he cried, having no hope in silence. "Arafel!"

A shadow loomed ahead of him. He flung himself aside, but it caught at him, and the stone warmed at his heart.

"Names are power," she said. "But you must use commands three times."

He caught her hand and held it, shut his

eyes, for a rush of shadows passed, and the Huntsman was among them. He thought that sight would scar him forever.

And the chill left him. He opened his eyes and they were walking through the mist into brightness, into sunlight, of green forest and meadows with pale flowers. He sank down on the grass, out of strength, and Arafel sat by him, gravely watching until he should have caught his breath.

"You are braver than wise," she said.

"I need your help," he said. "*They* need you."

"*They*." She flung herself to her feet, and indignation trembled in her voice. "Their wars are their own. You have seen. You have seen your choices. You have come back of your own will. Do you not know now how much we have to do with Men?"

He found no arguments. There was a grayness upon him like the grief of the fair folk themselves, when the world no longer suited them, nor they the world.

Her anger stilled. He felt it die from the stone. She knelt down by him and touched his face, touched his heart, which was still cold with the memory of the dogs.

"This," she said, touching the stone, "and iron—cannot bear one another. You know that now. You are wiser than you were. And when you are wiser still, you will know that they— have no part or peace with you."

"I have dreamed," he said, "and I know what

once you were. And I ask your help.—*Arafel,
Arafel—Arafel*, I ask your help for Caer Wiell."

Her face grew cold, and still. "Too wise," she
said. "Beware such invocations."

"Then take back your gift," he said. "There
is no heart in it."

"It *is* our heart," she said, and walked away.

He rose, looked about him, at hares which
sat solemnly beneath a white tree. He despaired, and shook his head, and would have
cast off the stone, but it was all his hope of
return to his own night. He had walked it
once; he began to walk it again, beyond the
silver trees, farther and farther into the mist,
for he sighted the direction true, and for whatever reason, the fear had gone.

His step never faltered, not in the direst and
strangest of the mist. Trees came clear to him,
and the very way to the room showed itself. He
saw it, a black cell before him in the grayness.
He entered it, and found walls about him once
more.

He sat still through the night. There were
no dreams. He slept a time and found the sun
coming up, washed himself and dressed and
came out into the hall, strangely numb of
terrors, even when he saw Scaga's man guard-
ing the hall, having watched him. He came
down into the hall where others gathered, and
silence fell.

THE SIDHE

"Is there place for me?" a voice asked softly. He looked. It was Arafel.

Others had risen from the table, a scraping of chairs and benches. Branwyn stared, her hands to her cheeks. Scaga laid hand to his sword, but no one drew. Arafel stood still, in forester's garments much mended and much faded. A sword hung at her side. Her pale hair was drawn back. She looked like a tall, slim boy.

"Long since I was here," she said in their silence. Somewhere on the walls alarms were sounding, summoning them to the attack. No one yet moved. "I am bidden aid you," she said. "I ask—do you wish that aid? Bid me aid you; or bid me go."

"We dare not take such help," said Meredydd.

"It is dangerous," said the harper.

"It is," said Arafel.

"Arafel," Ciaran said. "What danger?"

She turned her pale eyes on him. "The Daoine Sidhe had other enemies. There are things more than you see. Long and long it is since wars have reached into Eald."

"We die without your help," said Meredydd. "If help it is."

"Aye," said Arafel, "that might be true."

"Then help us," said Meredydd.

"Ask cost," said Scaga.

" 'Tis late for that," Arafel said softly. "Hist, do you not hear the alarms?"

"What costs?" Scaga said again.

"I am not of the small folk," Arafel said in measured words and cold. "I am not paid in a saucer of milk or a handful of grain. My reasons are my reasons. I speak of balances, Man, but it is late for that. My aid has been commanded, and I must give it."

"Then we will take it," said Scaga, with an anguished motion toward the door. "Out there, today."

"Give me time," said Arafel. "Hold against them in your own strength, and wait." She turned, looked on Branwyn and looked last on him, without anger, without passion at all. "Do not go out onto the walls," she said. "Stay within. Wait."

Her voice dimmed, and she did, so that there was only the stonework and a chair, and the silence after her.

"Arm!" Scaga shouted at the men, for still the alarm was sounding, and they had not answered it. "Come and arm!"

They ran. Ciaran stood still in the hall, feeling naked and alone. He realized the stone was in plain sight about his neck, and touched it, but it gave him nothing.

He looked back, into Branwyn's eyes. There was terror there.

"I knew her," Branwyn said. "We were friends."

"What happened?" he asked, disturbed to realize how meshed this place had been, forever, in the doings of Eald. "What happened, Branwyn?"

THE SIDHE

"I went into the forest," she said. "And I was afraid."

He nodded, knowing. There were then the two of them in the circle of fearing eyes. Lady Meredydd looked on them with a terror greater than all the rest, as if it were a nightmare she had shared. A daughter—who had walked in the forest, that they had gotten back again from Eald. Scaga knew, he too—who had seen a flinching from iron, and known clearly the name of the ill. It was terror come among them; but it had been there always, next their hearts.

"I am Ciaran," he said slowly, to hear the words himself, "Ciaran's second son, of Caer Donn. I lost myself in the forest, and I had her help to come here. But of the King, of your lord—I never lied. No."

No one spoke, not the ladies, not the harper. Ciaran went to the bench by the fire and sat down there to warm himself.

"Branwyn," Meredydd said sharply.

But Branwyn came and sat down by him, and when he gave his hand, took it, not looking at him, but knowing, perhaps, what it was to have walked the paths he took.

Arafel would come back. He trusted in this; and he remembered what Arafel had said that the others had not been willing to hear, except only Scaga, who might not have understood what she had answered.

Eald had dreamed in long silence; and Men asked that silence broken. *He* had done so, seeing only the power, and not the cost. He held tightly to Branwyn's hand, which was flesh, and warm, and he wondered if his hand had that solidness in hers.

War was coming, not of iron and blood. They were mistaken if they expected iron and fire of Arafel; and he had been blind.

He was not, now.

SEVENTEEN

The Summoning of the Sidhe

She walked quickly, and that was swiftly indeed, through the mists which rimmed her world, into the soft green moonlight on the silver trees. The deer and other creatures stared at her and came no nearer.

And when she had come to the heart of Eald, that grassy mound starred with flowers, and the circle of aged trees, then all of Eald hushed, even to the warm breeze which sported there. Moonlight glistened and glowed in the hearts of stones which hung on the tree of memory, and on the silver swords which hung nearby, and the armor and the treasures which held the magics of Eald. The magics slept, but for what sustenance they gave. Sleeping too, were the memories of all the faded Daoine Sidhe, which were the life of Eald.

She cast off the aspect she wore for Men, stood still a moment listening for the faintest of sounds, and then for no sound at all, but the whispering of elven voices. From one to the other stone she walked, touched them gently and drew their memories into life, so that none slept, not the least or the greatest.

And in the world of Men, Ciaran shuddered, and stared at the fire before them, feeling a stirring which shivered through the very earth. All that Men stood upon seemed like gossamer, threatening to tear.

"What is wrong?" asked Branwyn. "What do you feel?"

"The world is shaken," he said.

"I feel nothing," she said, as if to reassure him; but it did not.

Eald stirred. Arafel stood amid the grove and looked about her and listened; and at last went among the treasures of Eald and gathered up armor ages untouched, which had been hers. She put it on, mail shining like the moon itself, and took up her bow, and shafts tipped with ice-clear stone and silver. She took up her sword, and gathered the sword of Liosliath, his bow and all his arms. She climbed the knoll, laid down her burden, and sat down with her sword across her knees. She shut her eyes to Eald as it was, and listened to the stones.

"Eachthighearn," she whispered to the air,

THE DREAMSTONE · 249

and the silence trembled. A breeze began, which whispered down the green grass of the knoll and set the leaves to stirring and the stones to singing.

It moved farther, coursing narrowly through the trees, across the meadows, making flowers nod, and the hares which moved by moonlight looked up and froze.

It touched the waters of Airgiod, and skimmed them with a little shiver.

It blew among the trees the other side of Airgiod, and branches stirred.

"Eachthighearn: lend me your children."

The breeze blew along the distant flanks of hills, making them shiver, a nodding of grasses; and it traveled farther still.

Then it began to blow back again, through hills and forest, recrossing Airgiod's quiet waters, into meadows and into the grove, stirring the grasses of the knoll, with sighings of the swaying stones and a faint tang of sea breeze, recalling mist, and partings, and the cries of gulls.

Arafel shuddered in that wind, and the grayness beckoned. A taint of melancholy came over her, but she held fast to her stone, and opened her eyes and saw the grove as it was.

"Fionnghuala!" she called. "Fionnghuala! Aodhan!"

The breeze fled back again, laden with the green glamor of Eald, with sweet grass and shade, with summer warmth. It fled away, and the air grew still.

Then a wind began to blow returning, softly at first, and with greater and greater force in its coming, rattling the branches and making Airgiod's waters shiver, flattening the grasses and sweeping like storm into the grove, where the stones blazed with sudden light. The sky was clear, the stars pure, the moon undimmed, but storm crackled in the air, whipped the leaves, and Arafel sprang to her feet, holding the sword in her two hands. The force of lightnings stood about, shivered in her blowing hair and played about the swords in the trees. Thunder began, far away and growing in the wind, stirring like deepest song to the lighter chiming of the stones and the rush of leaves.

And with the wind came brightness in the night, one and the other, like moons coursing close to earth, with thunder in their hooves and moonlight for their manes ... above the earth they ran, together, as they had always coursed side by side.

"*Fionnghuala!*" Arafel hailed them. "Aodhan!"

The elven horses came to her in a skirling of wind, and the thunders bated as they circled her, as pale Fionnghuala stepped close and breathed in her presence with velvet nostrils shot with fire, gazed at her with eyes like the deer, wide and wonderful. Aodhan

snuffed the breeze and shook his head in a
scattering of light, stamped the ground and
shook it.

"No," said Arafel sadly. "He is not here.
But *I* ask, Aodhan."

The bright head bowed and lifted. She belted
her sword at her side and took up the arms
which had been Liosliath's. Fionnghuala came
to her, wickering. She seized the bright mane
in one hand and swung up, and Fionnghuala
stamped and turned, with Aodhan beside. The
pace quickened, and the wind scoured the
trees, swept the grass, a flicker of lightnings
crackling in the manes and in her hair.

"Caer Wiell," Arafel said to them, and
Fionnghuala ran, easily above the ground.
The mist lay before them, but the wind swept
into it, and lightnings lit it, making clear the
shapes long lost there, the upper course of
Airgiod, the shapes of faded trees. Shadows
were caught by surprise and fled in terror,
wailing down the wind as thunder took a
steady beat and mists were scattered.

Lightning blazed in Caer Wiell's court, danced
there, with thunder-mutterings . . . stood still,
and horses and rider looked on chaos, a gateway near to yielding, a scattering of men in
flight from the terror which had broken in
their midst. "Ciaran!" she called. "I am here!"

And Ciaran rose from his place beside the
fire, no more there, no more holding the hand

of Branwyn, whose voice wailed after him in grief.

He stood in the courtyard, with the stone burning like fire against his heart, with lightnings crackling about him and above him ... and the dreams were true.

Arafel slid down, a gleam of silver armor, and held out such armor to him in both her arms. He took it and put it on, buckled on the elvish sword, and all the while his heart was chilled, for the cold went from it to the center of him, and the lightnings surrounded them. The human day was murky, clouded; but they stood in otherwhere, and elven moonlight was cast on them, pale green; night went about them, an aura of storm, and of the two horses, he knew one for his.

"Aodhan," he named him. "Aodhan. Aodhan." And the horse came to him, stood waiting.

"Not yet," said Arafel, for there were others about them, human folk, who huddled against the wind, faces stark and frightened in the reflected glow, women and children and wounded men. They had no word to say to her; there were none from her to them. She walked toward the gate with Ciaran at her side and the elvish horses walked after.

"Scaga," Ciaran said, lifting his hand toward the wall. "Scaga," she repeated, and the old warrior looked down from the chaos on the walls, his face distraught.

THE SIDHE

"What you can do," Scaga said, "we beg you do."

"Beware, Scaga, what you have already asked. You have horsemen; ready them to ride with us, if they will."

The old warrior stood still several beatings of a mortal heart. He was wise, and feared them. But he called men to him, and came down the stairs, shouted orders at boys, and commanded the horses saddled. Arafel stood still, thoughtfully took her bow from off her shoulder, and strung it. She might, she thought, go to the wall, might aid them there. But iron arrows flew in plenty, and there was time enough for that.

"Mind," she said to Ciaran, "when you ride the shadow-ways, you are safe from iron—but you cannot strike at Men. Shift in and out of them; that is wisest."

"We can die," he said, "—can we not?"

"No," she said. "Not while you wear the stone. There is the fading. And there are other fates, Ciaran. Death is out there. Step into the shadow-ways and you will see him. Leave Men to me, where Men want killing. I am kinder than you know how to be. The arrows—save them: they are too dire for Men."

"Then what shall I do?"

"Ride with me," she said softly. "When one can do much—wisdom must guide the hand, or folly will. —Hist, they are ready."

Boys and men brought the horses of the keep,

handled, a clattering in the yard, and men ran from the defense of the walls and the gate to take them. Aodhan whickered softly and Fionnghuala saluted them too, and the mortal steeds herded together, ears pricked, nostrils straining. But Arafel walked among them, touched one and the other, named them their true names, and calmed them. "He is Whitetip," she told a rider; "and she is Jumper. Call them true and they are yours." The Men stared at her, but none durst question, not even Scaga, Whitetip's rider.

She looked toward the gate, which tottered beneath the ram. Fionnghuala stepped closer to her, dipped her head and shook it impatiently.

"Do not leave me," she bade Ciaran. "You have compelled my help. I do not compel: I ask."

"I am by you," he said.

"Scaga," she said. "Bid them open the gates. And quietly, to Ciaran: "Oftenest, Men see what they will, and cannot truly see us. Even these. Well for them they do not."

"Do I," he asked, "see you as you are?"

"I cannot know," she said. "But I know you. And you had power to call my name. One must see to do that."

He said nothing. She seized Fionnghuala's mane and swung to her back. He mounted Aodhan, and the horse suffered it with a shiver, a flaring and quivering of the nostrils, for it

THE SIDHE

was not his rider, but Ciaran knew the dream about his neck, of which Aodhan was part. Fionnghuala tossed her head, and the wind rose.

EIGHTEEN

The Battle
before the Gates

The gates yielded, a groaning and splintering of wood as the braces which held them were let go and the gates grated inward. Ciaran felt the horse dance aside, light as thistledown, ears still pricked toward the enemy: no need of harness, no need of holding. Aodhan picked up his feet and began to move as effortlessly as the wind which stirred about them, and his feet came down in the boom of thunder. Lightnings cracked, making hair and mane fly. Arafel rode beside him, as the white mare, tinted with the elven moon, paced stride for stride with Aodhan.

And the enemy who had rushed against the gate saw them, mirrored terror in lightning-lit faces, a soundless, horrid screaming. They brandished weapons, and still came on, impelled by hordes behind.

THE SIDHE

"Follow me!" said Arafel, and Fionnghuala flickered into shadow as she drew the silver sword. Ciaran clung to Aodhan and the horse strode into the shadow-ways.

Horror followed. A sickness passed him near: that was iron, a blade which passed through his substance, harmless in shadow-shape. Arafel thrust at that man; she flickered out of other-where in the midst of that thrust and back again: the silver blade had killed. The movements of Men and mortal horses were slow, and slowing still, as the elven horses strode their gliding and fearsome way, seeming to gallop but gaining less ground than speed. Ciaran had the sword in hand, but skill failed him—he struck, and failed his mark and struck again. The stone sang in his mind and something far colder than himself seized his heart; Aodhan sprang forward feeling it, and the thunder grew. There were other shapes with them, low, loping shapes of hounds, the taller blackness of horse and rider, which raced with them. Ciaran reached for his bow, overcome with horror.

"No," said Arafel. "Strike no blow at those."

Death drew away, parted from them in the course, and Ciaran looked back—saw Scaga and the other riders in that same slow movement of Men, cutting their way behind them. Cloaks and hair flew in frozen swirlings, with lightning flashes. Arafel called to him and the elven horses lengthened stride, began to move forward as well as swifter. Men passed by them, faster and faster, shadows through which they could move. Iron shivered past them with pain and poison, and the horses shied farther into otherwhere, flickered out again enough to see their way.

We are phantoms on the earth, Ciaran thought, and knew not which heritage *we* meant—for between those flickerings of otherwhere, like lightning-strokes, there was no army, only murky day, a strange placid landscape void of farms and wars and Men.

Yet not deserted. A horn sounded, braying, and came small folk scurrying from the hooves of the elven steeds—some fair and some foul, some direly misshapen. A weapon glanced from Ciaran's mail, and there was no fleeing. The thunder cracked and the horses leaped forward. Ciaran struck with the sword while it profited, saw Arafel herself beset by a tide of shadows which poured out of the thickening air. She vanished and he thought her slain, but the shadows poured after her into that nothingness.

"Go," he cried at Aodhan, and the horse leaped, following Arafel into mortal daylight. The shadows had not come through, or they hid, or transformed themselves. Arafel slew Men, a dire dream in which Ciaran's heart was chilled . . . I am of them, his heart cried; but another mind rose up in him, flowing into his limbs and his hands.

Give over, give over, the stone sang in his

THE SIDHE

heart, showing him his helplessness to wield these weapons.

He fought that voice, that one who strove to live, to come back. Aodhan ceased to obey him, raced wildly, while the wind grew and grew, while nightmares passed on either side. An anger rose in him at these ill-shapen things, these shadows that twisted into vision, the prickling of old hostility.

"Liosliath!" he heard them shout in rage; and the anger grew in him, lifted his arm, swelled in his heart. He shouted—he knew not what he cried. Aodhan leapt under him willingly, bore him along while his hands strung the elvish bow and he gathered up an arrow. The air swirled with storm: the arrow flew, ice-tipped, feathered with light. A horror shrieked and fled, and others coursed the winds. There was a light by him, which became Fionnghuala and her rider, and he saw Arafel's face calm and terrible as she sent shafts winging after his. Men ceased to matter. They were nothing. This was the war, these the enemy, old as earth, as they were old. Shapes fled before them, turning sometimes to strike and suffer wounds.

Suddenly they were alone, in a place gone gray and full of mists—They are fled, fled, the dream sang to him; and elsewhere, wherever he looked, was an iron-poisoned hush.

"Come," said Arafel, and shadow-shifted to a bloody and littered field. Rain came down and failed to reach them, pocked bloody puddles in the mire instead, drenched the broken human bodies and the shattered spears. They were in the midst of the field, with both sides drawn back for breath. Ciaran turned Aodhan and beheld Caer Wiell, with its men ranged before it afoot, the dozen riders still remaining to them standing huddled to the fore.

It was pause, not victory. It was regrouping, while the sky poured out its tears.

Another rider came treading above the mire of the center of the battlefield. He was a shape like a fragment of night, with his robes blowing in a wind counter of the wind which blew in the mortal realm. Lord Death stopped before them, leaned seemingly on the withers of the shadow-horse, and Ciaran shuddered, for in that shadow steed's head there was a pale hint of naked bone when the lightnings flashed.

"You are mad," said Death. "Go back. Cease this."

"I am bound," said Arafel. "They have invoked my aid."

Death straightened, and lifted a black sleeve toward the distant lines of the enemy. "*They* are there, come from under the hills to aid them. Do you not know? There are powers which have come to align with *them*."

"They would do so. But we are bound."

"There are my brother gods," said Death. "I bear you word from them; Withdraw, before worse is loosed."

The Sidhe

"Let them stay away," said Arafel. "Enough is amiss here."

"Go back," Death whispered. "If the Daoine Sidhe had all left this land, these fell things would never have come again."

"Because I have never gone away, dear youth— they have stayed to their hidings." She laughed and the shadow horse trembled. "Do you know *now* what watch I stand in Eald?"

Death and his horse stood still, bereft of answers. Ciaran gazed at the blackness, and Aodhan shifted and stamped, for things moved underfoot, and forces gathered.

"I do not bid you," Ciaran said to Arafel, although it was effort. "I know what has to be. I bound you to this. I release you. Give us over to Death, us and them, only so this ends."

Arafel gazed at him, and his skin prickled, for the lightnings stirred. "It is Men who lend them power," she said. "And your sight is truer than it was.—We are held to battle here on this field until the army yonder bids their own allies go back."

"And they who are winning—or losing—will not."

"That is so. When your mortal enemy has won, then their new allies will only be the stronger. They will go on, those powers; they will gather forces; they will sweep over all the world. Do you comprehend now, Man my cousin?"

"Forgive me," Ciaran whispered.

"It is heartsease you ask. I give you that. And I confess I had hope of more strength than we have in Caer Wiell. If we might rob the enemy of lives and human hands . . . but we have not strength enough."

"You have power unused," said Death. "Use it! Will you let them all break forth?"

"The cost of that too you know."

"Our need is *now*."

"That sacrifice will not kill them, only drive them hence for now. And what then, Lord Death? What in a hundred lifetimes of Men—when they go unwatched? You have no power over them, no more than over me. There is no hope that way. No, I will tell you what you must do: stay your hand from Caer Wiell. Our forces are too diminished as it is."

"I cannot," said Death, bowing his head. "I too am bound to what I do."

"My King," said Ciaran, "will come here, if only we can hold."

"Your King delays overlong," Arafel said quietly. "Wiser had you bound me to his aid, not to doomed Caer Wiell's. As it is, we are bound to serve and fall. And the cost of that fall you do not guess even yet."

"There was a battle," said Death, "a day ago. Trust me, that I know. There are still skirmishes; and that force is well-occupied in the hills, Man. Have no hope of them. This enemy has engaged them too, at the pass of Caerdale;

THE SIDHE

and all your King's strength cannot rout the enemy from those heights."

Ciaran listened. There seemed a gleam within that dark hood. There began a beating that was his heart, or Arafel's, or both. He laid a hand upon the stone at his throat, heard a whisper from it, felt an elvish presence that found courage to laugh at the thought that came into his mind; and Aodhan shifted to move at once.

"No," Arafel forbade him, but a light was in her eyes. "Wise you are, but that is no road for you, o Man. Yours to hold here. Where it serves Caer Wiell, *I* am free to ride."

"His human allies will all fall and the enemy will take him," Death said. His darkness became a nimbus about him. "I shall depart this field with all my forces. That much I can do."

"Go," said Arafel.

Death faded. There was only the rain, and then that stopped.

Arafel spoke to Fionnghuala. The white mare began to run. Aodhan whinnied after her, and pawed the ground, but stood fast.

And across the field the enemy began to gather their line.

Ciaran shivered. Beware, a voice in him whispered: you are only seeing Men. Others are closer.

"Liosliath," he said, holding up the stone, and shuddered, surrendering. "I shall stop being.

Wake. Wake, Liosliath. It is you they need now. Wake! your enemies are here!"

Cold fire spread from the stone. It frightened him, the power which spread through his limbs and the pride which drew breath and laughed, despising Men.

Aodhan wheeled then, and sped with long strides toward the battered lines of Caer Wiell, to pace delicately along before them. He saw Scaga's face, marred with a bloody slash; saw this fearless man give ground from him, saw others flinch. He flickered into otherwhere and saw the enemy gathered like a tide. He drew an arrow from his quiver and fired, saw the icy point lodge deep in a shadow which faded in torment.

And with the stone he drew on Eald, cast a glamor over all the force at his back, sheening them all in silver.

"Come," he called to them, and not he: the elf prince, who drew his sword and clapped his heels to Aodhan, the prince who knew well how to fence with iron, nothing reckoning the poisoned pain which whipped through his body when it must. Faster and faster Aodhan sped, and slower and slower the Men, while he brought the flickering elvish sword out of otherwhere, lodged in human flesh—gone again before human weapon could strike.

Yet none died. Enemies weakened, and human weapons hewed them ghastly wounds, and folk of Caer Wiell were spitted in turn, and did

not die, but kept hewing others, so long as
they had limbs which would move.

There was a wailing on the wind, a darkness.
He gathered strength against it and lightnings
flashed on monstrous shapes. Blows rained
against the silver mail; in rage he swept against
them, wounded them, and time and time again
Aodhan dropped into the mortal world, until
some of the dire things followed him there, and
undying Men stared in fear.

One of the Men was Scaga, whose anguished
look Ciaran knew, who still held his sword,
standing unhorsed in the mud. Then Ciaran's
heart was moved to pity, and he would have
taken the old warrior up, but Liosliath was
stronger, and Aodhan swept him on, skimming
the ground with thunder. The Caerbourne down
the hill flowed with blood. Saplings on the
banks were trampled. He used his sword against
Men wherever their ranks tried to stand, and
herded them and hurt them, though they would
not die. The light about him began to grow
paler and brighter, for human sun was sinking
into twilight, and elven sun was rising.

Then the dark things drew power more than
they had before, thrusting maimed human folk
forward to press against maimed Caer Wiell.

And now he was pressed back and back, for
the enemy was in all places, and on all sides,
converging on the ruined gate, and rending
those defenders who lagged in their retreat.

A Man stood by him, at Aodhan's shoulder:

Scaga. The old warrior shouted orders to his men and from the walls of Caer Wiell arrows flew, iron which the creatures hated as much as he. Some writhed in pain. Others crept up against the walls of the hold, and tore at the very stone.

And a wind grew in the east, and thunder.

"Arafel!" he cried.

She was there. He flickered into otherwhere and saw a light among the mists of the faded lands, with shadows rearing up between, caught and desperate. He held the gate against them, though his arm grew tired and Aodhan trembled beneath him. There was a thunder in the earth as well, and more and more human attackers added force to those who had come before. But a cry of dismay went up at the far side of that living tide, human screams and battle cries.

"Liosliath!" the call came down the wind, and he saw the flickering of the white mare and the gleam of Arafel's sword. Aodhan gathered himself and began to move, striding faster and faster.

And suddenly a shadow was beside him, a void shaped like horse and rider, and shapes like coursing hounds. Other dark riders had joined them, blacknesses as great as Death: and some who ran afoot, some like Men and some horned like stags.

Fionnghuala shone in the murk, and her rider no less than she: a pale and terrible

THE SIDHE

gleaming, her hair astream on the wind. "Liosliath!" Arafel hailed him, and he reached out a
hand as bright, caught hers across the gap, a
joy which burned and died, because of the dire
things about them.

Armies clashed in the dark and the storm,
and that noise was far from them. Dark things
leapt and attacked, slaying and being slain,
and wounded shapes climbed the winds. Lord
Death lifted the likeness of a horn and sounded
it, and the clouds increased as the dark horse
began to move; Aodhan paced the dark rider,
and Fionnghuala joined him. Side by side with
Death they rode, and the dogs bayed, coursing
more and more rapidly through the air. They
strode above the ground, and mounted the skirling winds. Aodhan threw his head and shook
himself and Arafel circled Fionnghuala out and
back again, hastening something fell and fugitive toward the dogs. Clouds tattered beneath
the hooves, and the thunders rolled. The horn
sounded yet again, and more and more riders
joined them, bearing banners like black cloud.
Armored Men, with darkened eyes set ahead
upon the quarry, and lances agleam in their
hands, rode on horses with eyes as dead as
theirs. The slain had gathered to hunt the newly
dead. Ciaran looked, and the Man in him
shuddered, for he knew some of these faces,
and he had loved no few of them. He saw a
cousin there; and a childhood friend, and another rider on a horse with a white-tipped ear—

"Scaga!" he called, but the rider coursed past, eyes dark, unheeding; and many a man of Caer Wiell followed after. The last turned and beckoned to him.

"Liosliath!" Arafel rebuked him. She held out her hand to him. Ciaran came, yielded to the elf prince, and Aodhan ran his gliding pace across the clouds, while the shadows fled.

They two turned back alone then, and rode the field in the human world, but the battle was done. Dark shapes slunk aside where they passed, sought refuge elsewhere, and vanished.

Men gathered at the gates of Caer Wiell, atop the hill. They rode quietly now, covering ground, a rush of wind about them, and had their weapons sheathed.

Then Arafel stopped, sat still on Fionnghuala, gazing toward the gates. "I am free," she said. " 'Tis done."

"Let us ride nearer," he begged her, for Donn had come riding in with lord Evald and the King's army; and there were the folk inside Caer Wiell. He ached to know how those he loved had fared.

"Would you see them?" Arafel asked him. "Aye, I do understand the bonds of kinship. Go."

She would not come inside the walls. He knew her pride, and ached for that as well. But Aodhan felt his will to go, and moved.

*   *   *

THE SIDHE

Men gave way before him, with fear on their faces. And when he had come as far as the gate, he saw lord Evald's banner, and Evald of Caer Wiell himself standing near it, giving orders to his men. Evald stopped and stared at him. And there kneeling by Evald's feet was Beorc, Scaga's son, who held Scaga's maimed and muddy body in his arms and mourned.

"He fought more than well," Ciaran said. Beorc looked up, and grief in his eyes became dread at what he saw. The look pained Ciaran like the iron, which ached more and more in the air about him, a taint in which it grew hard to breathe. Aodhan fretted to be away, and Ciaran rode farther, within the ruined gates, sought his father and Donnchadh and the moon banner of his own Caer Donn. Elf-sight found them quickly, and he stopped Aodhan by them in the swirl of Men in the courtyard.

They looked up at a strange rider and did not know him—surely they failed to recognize him, or they would never have had such a look of dread at the sight of him. He rode away from them, and Men shrank from his path in the crowded yard. "Stay," he bade Aodhan, slid down and walked among the Men, among his own, past cousins of his, seeing everywhere that look he dreaded.

He moved elsewhere, a reaching of the heart, a shifting, and found himself in the stone hall of Caer Wiell, by the fireside, where Lady

Meredydd and Branwyn stood. Their eyes showed no less fear than the others had.

"They are well," he said, holding the stone at his heart to ease the ache in it. "Your lord is home. You are safe. But Scaga is dead."

He wept in telling it, not having wished to weep, and began to fade. But Branwyn called his name and held him by it. She tried to come to him, a mortal yearning. He reached and took her hand to help her, but she could not come the way he could. He kissed her fingers, and kissed her brow, and stayed a time in the room with them.

Lord Evald came, and the King with him. To the King, Ciaran knelt, while Laochailan's young eyes regarded him with that dread others turned on him.

"Welcome sight," the King he had loved said of him; but with the lips, not with the heart. And Evald, lord Evald, who was Eald's near and knowing neighbor, gave him a look as bleak and unwelcoming—then came and offered him an embrace.

No other human dared, not his own father or brother, when they had come up the stairs into the hall, all clattering with armor. "Ciaran," his father said, and gazed on him with a bleak, hag-ridden stare. Donnchadh started a step toward him, but his father held his arm and prevented him. Then Donnchadh's face became like a stranger's to him, grim and mournful.

They have always known, Ciaran thought, both of them have always known what is in our blood. He recalled the elvish moon which had been Caer Donn's banner for years out of memory, and was heartstricken at such a look as Donnchadh gave him.

"We are going back," his father told the King then without looking at him, as if he had not been there. "We have our own cares, too long neglected."

"Go," the King bade him; so his father and his brother went their way from the hall, not to linger long near Eald, and never looked back.

Ciaran stood wounded, looked last at Branwyn, who looked at him, and in his pain he wished himself away, in the cold air, in the mist, the deserted shadow-ways.

He came back into the mortal night in the courtyard after some time had passed, where all was quieter than it had been.

He walked outside the riven gates, where the horror of the field was honest and undiminished. "Aodhan," he said quietly, and a wind gusted as the horse moved out of the night toward him, slow peals of thunder, a blazing like the noon of elvish sun. He stroked the white neck and thought of his home in the hills, at Caer Donn. He might go there, might— once—go there, greet his mother and his kin, see the things he had known, bring them word days before his father and Donnchadh and the men could come and tell them—before that place was closed to him forever, before—so many things. Aodhan could carry him.

He touched the stone at his throat. "Arafel," he said.

It was another presence which came to him instead, which touched his heart far more gently than it had ever done, with elvish brightness. There was pride—always that; but this time the touch was warm. "Man," it whispered; and there was the roar of the sea and the cries of gulls. *"Man."*

Only that he said, the elven prince, and it sufficed.

NINETEEN

The End of It All

He came, but not alone, and that surprised her—in plain good clothes, and with Branwyn tramping along with him through the brambles, her golden hair tangled with twigs. He wore the sword and carried the bow and a pack which clearly burdened him. She watched them, and would have reached out to help them, but she sensed the fear in Branwyn, and could not have helped, no more than he could: Branwyn was doomed to the thorns.

They reached the dancing-ring. He called her in his mind, and she came, smiling sadly at the pain in his eyes, and looked then at Branwyn, who managed to look back at her.

"I have brought Aodhan back," Ciaran said.

"Swiftest to have ridden," said Arafel.

"Branwyn tried."

"Ah," she said in pity, and again met Branwyn's blue eyes. "You might have."

Fear looked back at her, but something like the child struggled behind it. "I wanted to."

"That is much," said Arafel.

A wind had risen. She sensed Aodhan near, but it was Ciaran who had the summoning of him. Ciaran held out a hand, and the horse stepped into mortal sunlight, aglow with the elvish moon. Small thunders rumbled in the glade, and lightnings flickered. Ciaran stroked Aodhan's neck, and whispered his name and bade him go. The thunder clapped and the horse was gone, that swiftly, and perhaps something of Ciaran's heart went with him; he had that look.

Then Ciaran knelt down and unbound the pack which he had brought, and took the sword and bow and laid them atop it all the shining armor at her feet.

"Thank you," Arafel said, and the gifts faded.

"I thank you," Ciaran said. "I must thank you. But—do you understand?—I have carried them as far as I can. I have seen things—I shall always see them. They are enough."

"I know," she said.

He rose, and reached last for the chain about his neck.

"No," she said. "That, you must keep."

"I cannot," he said. He drew it off, and offered it to her hands, his own hands trembling.

"It is your protection."

"Take it."

"And Branwyn's too. Do you even hope to get from out this forest without it? Would you see her hunted too?"

That struck deep. Ciaran's hands fell; but Branwyn took his arm.

"I knew that too," said Branwyn, and there was more of sense in her blue eyes than there had ever been. "But I am here. And we will walk out again."

"Please," Ciaran said, offering the stone yet again. "I am a Man, and when he comes, that is the way of Men, is it not? But if I keep this, there is no hope for me."

Arafel took it then, unwilling, and her lips parted in shock at the strength that had come to it, and the presence in it which was indeed almost beyond bearing.

"Ah," she said, folding it to her heart. She looked on him with tears. "You have given me a gift, o Man. And now there is nothing you have left me to give you."

"A blessing," he said, "for us. That I will take."

"Few Men have ever asked it of the Daoine Sidhe."

"I ask."

She kissed him then, and kissed Branwyn. "Go," she said.

They went, hand in hand, and she walked behind them, the shadow-ways, unseen. They had trouble in the going, took scratches of the thorns, and climbed high places and limped on unexpected stones; shadows hissed at them, but fled quickly when she bade them gone.

And at last it was New Forest, and Arafel stood upon the flat rock and watched them down the slope, toward the Caerbourne, and Caer Wiell.

A blackness settled near her. She frowned at it.

"Give them a little," she asked. "Only a little time."

"We were allies," Death said. "Should I have so short a memory? I shall wait. As for Branwyn—she was always mine."

Again she frowned.

"I have another face," he said.

She drew herself up and laid a hand on her sword. "Beware of me, Lord Death; I know your name; and the day I see you as you are, you are yourself in peril. Do not tempt me."

"You have asked a favor," he said.

"Aye," she said more softly, anger fallen. "That I have."

"He may come here if he wills; and she may. He will die abed, years hence. That, I give to him."

"Then I forgive you," she said, "other things."

She left him then, and walked her own way, from Airgiod's quiet rim, to the moonlit grove.

Fionnghuala was there, and Aodhan. "Go," she bade them. "You are free."

They did not go; and they were free to choose

THE SIDHE

that too. They stayed near, and the grove breathed with wind and memories.

"Liosliath," she said, holding the stone near her heart.

He was aware. There *was* another place but this. She held it close and walked amid the silver trees.

Eald was smaller. But it had held. She found that place at the edge of Eald, hers and not quite hers, and the Gruagach scampered into hiding, remembering ancient quarrels—but he fared well, and so did all he cared for. The fields were safe. She preferred the earth no iron had delved, the lands shadowed with her trees—but she took care now of lands far wider than Eald, so that the lands of Men had rarely seen such a year, in which no planting failed. It cost her. She did all she could to mend what war had done, and stretched her care as far as it could go. Long ago she had chosen this woods and kept it—but now it had neighbors she valued, with special poignancy, that they were brief and brave and given to doing as they would. She had never known why she watched, except for pride, not to yield forever what once the Sidhe had been; but now it was for love.

Yet one day, one day she almost despaired, so much of Eald she had given away. She came for comfort to that heart of her wood and walked there listening to the stones, her head bowed in a weariness almost too much to bear.

So she found it, a tiny thing unlooked for at

her feet. A branch, she thought, had fallen
from the silver trees, which had never happened in any wind that blew—so, she thought
as she bent down by it, Eald had at last begun
to die, from the heart outward.

Then she cast herself to her knees in wonder—
for the sprig was rooted in the ground, thrusting up from the earth with silver leaves all
delicately veined, the first new life in Eald
since the dimming of the world.

AFTERWORD

On Names

Ealdwood is a place in faery and has like all such places an indefinite geography. The nomenclature is Celtic and Welsh, with a touch of the Old English, so this particular corner of faery in language and in spirit sits at some juncture of lands where there has been much coming and going of various peoples, likeliest some corner just above Wales, a lovely and ancient place. In this world the speakers of the English are farthest east; the Welsh to the south; and the speakers of the Celtic tongues have their homes farthest seaward—perhaps they had come from the sea.

As for the elves, they have generally Celtic names, or the Celtic is very like elvish: or what it once was.

Certain of the names like Arafel and Evald

which appear early and often, show a different orthography, being somewhat older in the story, and here retained in mercy to the reader, and in further sympathy to the reader who may never have dealt with any of these tongues, the following table may provide some aid, and some delight as well, since the names of Eald are, if one knows how to look at them, our own.

There are many sounds to be passed over very lightly: the reader skilled in languages may come closest to the ancient way of saying them just by the hint of them passing over the tongue. But this was very long ago and accents change even over one hill and the other, let alone in and out of faery. For most readers who only wish to read without tripping on the words, this table will give little hint of these almost silent sounds, paring them away until only the simplest version is left. C will denote the words that are Celtic; W the Welsh; OE the English.

In general, in the Celtic words, be it noted, mh and bh are the sound we call v; ch is breathed, if possible, as in familiar lo*ch*, a word for lake (but k will do);-gach has often by our day gone to the sound of a hard -gy; and the profusion of vowels has generally a single simple sound at the heart.

In the Welsh most notably -dd- is -th-.

In the English, easiest to render ae- as simple e-, and to treat hr- as r-.

On Names

Where a name has a more familiar form, it will be given in capitals.

And if for any reader this small list provokes further curiosity, Celtic, Welsh, and old English reference works are not that difficult to find. A good place to begin is, after all, with names, the -nesses and -hams and -denes and -eys that come off modern tongues as if they had no meaning in themselves. Names do have power, after all, that of conjuring images of places we have not seen.

aelf (elf) OE an elf

Aelfraeda (elf red a) OE from aelf [elf] and raeda [counsel]

aesc (esh) OD ash

Aescbourne (esh burn) OE ash brook: ASHBURN

Ascford (esh ford) OE ash ford: ASHFORD

Aesclinn (esh linn) OE ash pool: ASHLIN

Airgiod (ar gi ud) C silver

An Beag (an beg) C small

Aodhan (a o dan) C rascal

ap (ap) W son of

Arafel (ar a fel) C from AOIBHEIL (a o ev al) joyous

Ban (ban) C fair, pale

Banain (ban en) C fair; BANNEN

Bebhinn (bev in) C BEVIN

Beorc (burk) OE birch: BURKE

Beorhthramm (burt ram) OE: bright raven; BERTRAM

Boglach (bog lach) C marsh
bourne (burn) OE stream
brad (brad) OE broad
Bradhaeth (brad heath) OE broad heath
Branwyn (Bran win) W from BRONWEN (bron win) white breast
Cadawg (ca-doc) W warrior; CADDOCK
Cadhla (ca ly) C fighter; CALEY
caer (ker) W stronghold
Caer Damh (ker dav) C stag keep
Caer Luel (ker lel) OE castle keep: CARLISLE
Caer Wiell (ker well) OE spring keep
Caerbourne (ker burn) castle brook
Caoimhin (ku EV in) C kindly: KEVIN
Carraig (KAR rak) C standing stone
Caerbhallain (KER va len) C victor: CARROL (an)
Ciaran (KEE ran) C twilight: KIERAN
Cinhil (kin il)
Cinnfhail (kin vel) C head
Coinneach (ko en nach) C moss: KENNETH
Conmhaighe (kon vay) C hound: CONWAY
Cuilean (kul an) C cub: QUILLAN
Dalach (da lach) C advisers DALEY
damh (dav) C stag
Daoine Sidhe (thee na Shee) C the People of Peace; the folk of Faery. Often powers felt to be dangerous and perhaps ill-wishing are named by names felt to be quite contrary to their natures, to avoid calling them up accidentally or offending them by mentioning their true names; again, the feeling is that the true name

is not for using. And of course the Daoine Sidhe are not likely to give the true name of all their kind for common use. Other names are the FAIR FOLK, for much the same reason. SIDHE applies to many kinds of creature: the Gruagach by some extension is one of the Sidhe and so are some things very much worse to look on. But the Daoine Sidhe are the highest of their kind.

Diarmaid (der mit) C free: DERMOT

Diomasach (dem sey) C proud: DEMPSEY

Donn (don) C brown

Donnchadh (don cad) C brown tartan: DUNCAN

Dryw (drew) W sight: DREW

Dubh (du) C black

Dubhlachan (du la han) C dark; DOOLAHAN

Dun na h-Eoin (dun na hey win) C tower of birds

each (ek) C horse

Eachthigtern (ek ti arn) C lord of horses

ead (ed) OE noble

eald (eld) OE old

Evald (ev ald) OE fr. AECWEALD, oak wood

Fearghal (fir gal) C valorous man: FARREL

Feochadan (fo ka dan) C thistle

Fionn (fee an) C fair: FINN

Fionnbharr (fin var) C fairhair

Fionnghuala (fin el a) C white shoulder: FIN-ELLA

Fitheach (fay ak) C raven

Flann (flan) C red

Glas (glass) C gray

Gruagach (gru gy) fr. C: hairy. The word has scattered meanings. As one of the Sidhe, this is one of the working sort who performs homely tasks.

Haesel (hay sel) OE hazel: HAZEL

haeth (heath) OE heath: HEATH

Holen (ho len) OE holly: HOLLIN

Hrothhramm (roth ram) OE famous raven

Laochailan (la ok lan) C hero: LACHLANN

linn (lin) OE pool: LYNN

lios (li-ess) C Sidhe fort

Liosliath (liess-lia) C gray Sidhe fortress: LESLEY

Lioslinn (liess-lin) C Sidhe fort lake

Lonn (lon) C strong: LONN

Meara (mer a) C wild laughter

Meredydd (me re dith) W sea: MEREDITH

Muirne (murn a) C hospitality; MYRNA

Niall (ne al) C hero: NEAL

Ogan (o gan) C youth

righ (ree) C king

ruadh (ro ak) C red; red deer

Ruaidhrigh (ru a ree) C red king or deer king; RORY

Sgeulaiche (skel ly) C storyteller; SKELLY; SCULLY

Siobrach (sov rak) C primrose

Siolta (shel ta) C waterfowl

Skaga (skag a) C stand of trees; SHAW

Taithleach (tul ly) C experienced; TULLY

ON NAMES

Tiamhaidh (tiv ak) C drear
tighearn (ti arn) C lord
wiell (well) OE spring
wulf (wolf) OE wolf

DAW

More Top-Flight Science Fiction and Fantasy from
C.J. CHERRYH

DAW

SCIENCE FICTION MASTERWORKS FROM THE INCOMPARABLE C.J. CHERRYH

DAW

MAGIC TALES FROM THE MASTERS OF FANTASY